The Body Snatchers Affair

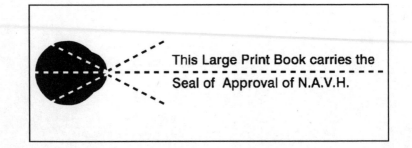

This Large Print Book carries the
Seal of Approval of N.A.V.H.

A CARPENTER AND
QUINCANNON MYSTERY

THE BODY SNATCHERS
AFFAIR

MARCIA MULLER
BILL PRONZINI

THORNDIKE PRESS
A part of Gale, Cengage Learning

GALE
CENGAGE Learning·

Farmington Hills, Mich • San Francisco • New York • Waterville, Maine
Meriden, Conn • Mason, Ohio • Chicago

GALE
CENGAGE Learning®

LIBRARY OF CONGRESS CATALOGING-IN-PUBLICATION DATA

Muller, Marcia.
    The body snatchers affair : a Carpenter and Quincannon mystery / Marcia Muller and Bill Pronzini. — Large print edition.
        pages cm. — (A Carpenter and Quincannon mystery) (Thorndike Press large print mystery)
    ISBN 978-1-4104-7674-6 (hardcover) — ISBN 1-4104-7674-X (hardcover)
    1. Women detectives—Fiction. 2. Missing persons—Investigation—Fiction. 3. Large type books. I. Pronzini, Bill. II. Title.
PS3563.U397B63 2015
813'.54—dc23   2014045576

Published in 2015 by arrangement with Tom Doherty Associates, LLC.

Printed in the United States of America
1 2 3 4 5 6 7 19 18 17 16 15

For Patsy McCord Jones

1
SABINA

Hacquette's Palace of Art, on Post Street near Market, was one of San Francisco's most fashionable restaurants. Not only was the menu extensive and the cuisine reputed to be outstanding, it housed a considerable number of preeminent works of art — fine paintings, marble carvings, hammered silver plaques and cups. Many different types of curios adorned the walls as well, among them redwood burls and other uniquely shaped and colored wooden items. An elaborate rococo bar occupied one side of the large dining room; tables covered with immaculate white linen were arranged throughout, as well as upon a balcony opposite the bar.

This October Tuesday evening Sabina sat with her escort, Carson Montgomery, at one of the intimate balcony tables. Although her cousin Callie French had spoken of the Palace of Art to her, she had never before had occasion to dine there. Carson, however, judging from the fawning attentions of the maître d' and the headwaiter, was something of a regular customer. Not that that was any surprise; he was a member of the socially prominent Montgomery family and one of the city's more eligible bachelors, and well-known at a number of first-class restaurants and other elegant gathering places.

He was a handsome man, clean-shaven except for long sideburns, his hair curly brown. His most striking feature, the one that had drawn Sabina to him initially and continued to command her attention whenever they were together, was his eyes. Bright blue, lively, interested, gentle, and kind. Yet with the type of inner fire that proclaimed him a man of action who would respond quickly to the threat of danger.

So much like Stephen's eyes . . .

Like Stephen in other ways, too? Perhaps, she thought as she watched Carson confidently ordering for both of them, but she didn't know him well enough to make any definite judgments. Certainly there were no professional similarities. He was a metallurgist who had spent several years working in the rough-and-tumble goldfields of the Mother Lode and who was currently employed by Monarch Engineering, while Stephen had been one of the Pinkerton Detective Agency's most capable operatives. Her late husband had also been the most capable, most passionate man she had ever known. Before Carson, the only other she'd encountered who possessed similarly admirable qualities was John Quincannon. But her esteem for her business partner was purely professional, or so she kept telling herself, and her feelings for Carson were still uncertain. It was Stephen who remained uppermost in her thoughts and her heart and always would.

She had met him in Chicago, where she'd been born. Although her father also had been a Pinkerton man, she'd been allowed little knowledge of his profession while growing up, being steeped in the conventions deemed proper for a middle-class young lady. By her eighteenth birthday, she had grown thoroughly sick of afternoon teas, quilting parties, and silly evening soirees, and longed for a more exciting, adventurous life. When her father died shortly afterward, from complications of gout, she made up her mind to follow his career path and applied for a secretarial position with the Pinkerton agency. From the first she'd shown aptitude for detective work, perhaps inherited from her father, and it was not long before she was promoted to the status of "Pink Rose," as the agency's female operatives were called. Stephen, already an established Pinkerton operative, had been transferred to the Chicago office six months later. Their courtship had been as ecstatic as it was swift.

Within a year of their marriage, they were transferred together to the Denver office. They'd had five years together there, five short years of sharing private moments and occasionally working together before his life was snuffed out, through no fault of his own, in a shooting scrape with a band of outlaws. His death had devastated her, thrust her into a deep depression that had nearly cost her her livelihood. A friend had helped rid her of the shackles of grief and self-pity by urging her to resume her career. This she'd done, throwing herself tirelessly into her work.

If it hadn't been for an undercover assignment in Silver City, Idaho, she might still be living in Denver and working as a Pink Rose. For it was in Silver City, while posing as a milliner (though she knew little about the creation of hats), that she'd met John, then a near-alcoholic treasury agent investigating a counterfeiting case. Their liaison

10

had altered the course of both their lives. On his return to San Francisco he had sworn off demon rum, left the Secret Service to open his own detective agency, and persuaded her to relocate and join him as an equal partner. She'd never regretted the move. Carpenter and Quincannon, Professional Detective Services, was now a well-established and prosperous enterprise.

She led a full life in her new home, free of the strictures placed by the era's Victorian standards on single, married, and widowed women. As a professional detective, she was able for the most part to do as she chose, associate with whom she pleased, without male interference (except John's now and then). Her apartment on Russian Hill was a cozy haven; her cat, Adam, a pleasant companion; and Callie and her husband, Hugh, had provided an entrée into local society.

It was Callie who had pressed her to attend the dinner party, "just a few of our more interesting acquaintances," at which she'd met Carson. Like most of Callie's "small dinner parties," this one had mushroomed into a soiree complete with an orchestra, uniformed servants bearing trays laden with canapés, and a score of her plump, bejeweled friends and their well-fed

11

husbands. Callie was an inveterate match-maker; she invariably invited one or more eligible bachelors in the hope of piquing Sabina's interest. None had until Callie practically forced Carson onto her, and she'd looked into those bright blue eyes, Stephen's eyes. When he'd taken her hand, she'd felt a tingling electric current pass between them.

Since then they had dined four times at elegant restaurants, taken a buggy ride through Golden Gate Park, and held lively conversations on all manner of subjects. He was attentive, interesting, possessed a keen sense of humor, and had been a perfect gentleman — in fact, he hadn't even attempted the liberty of a good-night kiss. She enjoyed his company, felt comfortable with him. Still, she was hesitant about the courtship — if indeed that was what it was — and not quite sure why. Stephen and her memories of their time together, yes. John was part of the reason, too, in spite of her vow to keep their relationship on a professional-only basis. But there was something else that she couldn't quite define. . . .

Carson was saying something to her. She blinked, refocused her attention on him across the table.

"Woolgathering?" he asked with a smile. "Or were you thinking about one of your investigations?"

"Oh . . . neither, actually. I was thinking of adopting another cat." This was not really a fib. She had indeed been considering another feline adoption; she was absent from her apartment a good deal, and Adam would be happier, she felt, if he had a companion.

"One isn't enough for you?"

"I'm not enough for him."

"Well, then. It so happens a relative of mine is looking to place a litter of kittens. All black, wiggly, and charming."

"Really? Perhaps you could arrange an interview."

"An interview . . . with cats?"

"Each has its own personality. I could determine which meshes best with Adam's and mine."

Carson nodded and said he would be happy to make the arrangement. Just then goblets of wine arrived — an excellent French Chablis. He raised his and made a toast, as he had at their previous dinner engagements. This one, however, was a touch more personal.

"To us," he said. "And the rosiest of futures."

Sabina felt her smile dim slightly as she touched her glass to his. He seemed to want their relationship to move forward more rapidly than she did. She simply didn't know him well enough. Nor was she at all sure that she wanted or needed intimacy with any man. It had been more than four years since Stephen's death and though tempted a time or two since — by John, of all possible suitors — she had remained celibate. The passion she had shared with her late husband could never be matched, of that much she was certain.

Fortunately, Carson made no more statements of a personal nature. While they ate their first course — plump, juicy South Bay oysters on the half shell — he asked what sort of cases Carpenter and Quincannon, Professional Detective Services, were presently working on.

"Oh, a small matter of stolen checks, a breach of contract suit, a larcenous servant. The only recent one of interest came to us just this afternoon."

"And that would be?"

"Well, it's confidential. All I can tell you is that it has a Chinatown connection."

"Ah. The trouble brewing there? The stolen body of the late tong president? The

14

newspapers have been full of those stories lately."

"Yes, they have. But of course I can't reveal the specifics."

"Of course. The situation appears to be potentially volatile, however. I hope your investigation won't put you in harm's way."

"No. It's John's case more than mine." Sabina felt a momentary thrust of concern, for John had gone to prowl about China-town tonight on behalf of their client, the wife of an opium-addicted attorney named James Scarlett, and the rancid byways of the Quarter could be dangerous after dark. She banished the concern by saying, "He's well able to take care of himself."

"He, too, must be a very good detective."

"Yes. He is."

"When will I have the pleasure of meeting him?"

Not any time soon, Sabina thought wryly. John was a very good detective, yes, but he was also infatuated with her, in a way that went beyond what had seemed at first to be typical male lechery, and ridiculously jealous as a result. She hadn't told him about Carson, nor would she until — if — their relationship progressed beyond its present casual stage. He would grumble and growl if he knew, and if he and Carson came face-to-face, sparks were liable to fly and there was no telling what might happen.

"I really can't say," she said. "He's quite busy these days."

"Try to arrange it, won't you? You speak so often and so well of him that my curiosity has been aroused."

Oh, Lord. Now he's *the jealous one!*

"Yes," she lied, "I'll try."

Carson smiled and reached across the table to entwine his fingers with hers. She felt the familiar electricity as his blue eyes, Stephen's eyes, gazed into hers. But then the uncertainty came again. What was it about this attractive, cultured man that bothered her? A reserve, perhaps, that piqued her detective's instincts and made her wonder if he was exactly the man he seemed to be; if there might be some part of him he deliberately kept hidden.

That seemed unlikely, for his life had been chronicled in detail by Callie, and in a profile in the *Sunset Limited.* His reputation was impeccable, as was that of the entire Montgomery family. What could he possibly have to hide? Unless it was something from his roving days in the Mother Lode . . .

While they dined on crab cakes, she encouraged him to talk about his mining experiences. He'd mentioned them before,

16

but only in a general way. He was forthcoming enough tonight, but in a way that made Sabina think he might be holding back, reluctant to provide specific details.

"By the time I left my last job in Nevada County," he said, "the rough-and-ready years were over and the area was showing signs of civilization — churches and church socials, quilting bees, even a small art museum. The miners imported their women, you know, and with respectable ladies came polite society. Of course there were still a disproportionate number of saloons and houses of ill repute."

"You were quartered in Grass Valley?"

"For a short time, yes. In the Holbrooke Hotel, as fine a hostelry as one could hope for in the Sierra foothills. None of the other counties I worked in offered such satisfactory accommodations."

"What exactly was it you did in the mines?"

"Principally, study and report on the quality of the ore to be extracted from them. Most were opened in mid-century, and many had been played out by that time, or were capable of yielding only low-grade ore, but a few of the larger mines continued to produce substantial amounts of gold. Whenever new veins were discovered or old ones threatened to play out, I was employed by the owners to assess them."

"It must have been interesting work."

"Only to a metallurgist." His smile was a trifle crooked, she thought. "But the places . . . French Camp, for instance. Not only was it a first-rate mining town, but also the terminus of the first long-distance telephone lines in the country. And Downieville in Sierra County, once the fifth largest town in the state. It almost became the capital of California, you know, losing to Sacramento by a mere ten votes."

"Did you have any adventures in those days?"

"Adventures?"

"At the mines or in the towns. Encounters with desperadoes, that sort of thing."

A frown darkened Carson's features, tightened the corners of his mouth. "No."

"Nothing at all exciting or dangerous?"

"Nothing at all," he said, and immediately changed the subject.

Now Sabina was convinced that he was holding back, concealing some unpleasantness in his past. There was nothing necessarily wrong in that; most people at one time or another had done or been caught up in something they preferred to keep to themselves. Still, being cautious and inquisi-

18

tive by training and nature, she couldn't help wondering if Carson's secret indicated a dark side to his nature.

The main course he had ordered for them was *boeuf bourguignon*. He consulted the wine list, then summoned their waiter to order a bottle of Bordeaux. While he was doing this, Sabina happened to glance down and across the busy dining room toward the long ornate bar. A tall, angular man in evening dress who stood at the near end, directly opposite their balcony table, was staring intently up at her. Startled, she peered back at him. He was familiar . . . too familiar.

No, it can't be him!

But it was. Even at a distance, even outfitted like Carson and the other male diners, that lean, hawklike countenance was unmistakable. And when he realized that she'd caught his riveted attention, he turned abruptly and hurried away toward the entrance. A moment later he was gone.

Sabina was nonplussed, to say the least. The last time she'd seen the Englishman who claimed to be the famous detective, Sherlock Holmes, had been less than a month ago. Outlandishly dressed in one of his inexplicable disguises, he'd accosted her on a streetcar on her way home to give her what had turned out to be valuable information on related cases she and John were investigating. He'd claimed to be involved in some mysterious undercover work of his own, and she'd thought — hoped — that would be the last she would see of him. But here he was again. Coincidence that he'd turned up like a bad penny on the same night she was dining at the Palace of Art? She fervently hoped so. John would be furious if the "crackbrain," as he called the bogus Sherlock, once more attempted to insinuate himself into their lives.

The *boeuf bourguignon* and the Bordeaux were both excellent. As was the gateaux Sabina ordered for dessert. Her appetite had always been prodigious, and she was one of those fortunate individuals who never gained an ounce no matter how much rich food she consumed.

She and Carson lingered over coffee. He was something of a raconteur and more than once he made her laugh out loud with stories that ranged from the droll to the mildly outrageous. By the time they left the restaurant, she felt comfortable with him again, her earlier fears of a possible dark side to his nature temporarily dispelled.

Outside, the night was chilly. Sabina drew her angora wrap tightly about her as Carson went to engage the first in a line of three waiting hansom cabs, and glanced casually about the vicinity while she waited. A few pedestrians, passing conveyances . . . and a dark figure lurking in a doorway a short distance away.

Oh, no!

She kept a narrowed eye on the doorway as Carson returned to take her elbow and guide her to the hansom. Just as she took the first step up, she saw the figure emerge and had a clear look at him in the glow of a streetlight as he hurried into the next hack in line.

Oh, yes, *drat him. The bogus Mr. Holmes.*

The hack containing him took every turn hers and Carson's did on the way to the lower flank of Russian Hill, following a relatively short distance behind. Sabina confirmed this by three brief glances through the rear window.

Now she was bemused as well as irritated. Why on earth would the crackbrain want to spy on her? It couldn't be for usual reasons men followed women; like the genuine Sherlock Holmes, he seemed to have little if any romantic interest in the female sex. But neither could she imagine any other reason for his not so covert surveillance. Of course, the man wasn't in his right mind, but there

21

had always been method in his mad behavior before. The previous cases of hers and John's that he'd intruded into, with rather startling results, had been of considerable importance and notoriety. None of the agency's current investigations had any such significance, except possibly the one involving the unrest in Chinatown and that had come to them only today.

When their hansom arrived at her flat, Carson escorted her to the front door. The street was sufficiently well lighted for her to note that the trailing hack drew up less than half a block behind. At the door, Carson was once again the perfect gentleman; he took her hand, kissed it, said that it had been a splendid evening, and invited her to attend a dramatic performance at the Baldwin Theatre on Saturday evening. She accepted tentatively and a little distractedly, and he smiled, bowed, and left her.

Sabina went inside and shut the door, only to open it again a few inches and peer out. She watched Carson climb back into the hansom they had shared, the driver crack his whip smartly to start them moving again along the cobbles. Watched the Englishman's hansom jerk into motion, following until both were out of sight.

This was even more disconcerting. From

the look of things, the would-be Sherlock hadn't been spying on her after all.

The person he was spying on was Carson Montgomery.

2
QUINCANNON

In his twenty years as a detective John Quincannon had visited a great many strange and sinister places, but this September night was his first time in an opium den. And not just one — four of the scurvy places, thus far. Four too many.

Cellar of Dreams, this one was called. Supposedly one of the less odious of the reputed three hundred such resorts that infested the dark heart of San Francisco's Chinatown in this year of 1895. (Another Caucasian-generated myth like the one that claimed the existence of a subterranean honeycomb of secret rooms and passages throughout the Quarter; in actuality the number of opium dens was well under a hundred.) Located in Ross Alley, it was nonetheless a foul-smelling cave full of scurrying cats and yellowish-blue smoke that hung in ribbons and layers. The smoke seemed to move lumpily, limp at the ends;

its thick-sweet odor, not unlike that of burning orange peel, turned Quincannon's seldom-tender stomach for the fourth straight time.

"The gentleman want to smoke?"

The question came in a scratchy singsong from a rag-encased crone seated on a mat just inside the door. On her lap was a tray laden with nickels — the price of admittance. Quincannon said, "No, I'm looking for someone," and added a coin to the litter in the tray. The statement, he thought corrosively, was no doubt one she had heard a hundred times before. Cellar of Dreams, like the other three he'd entered, was a democratic resort that catered to Caucasian "dude fiends" — well-dressed ladies and diamond-studded gentlemen from the upper stratum of society — as well as to Chinese coolies with twenty-cent *yenshee* habits. Concerned friends and relatives would come looking whenever one of these casual, and in many cases not so casual, hop smokers failed to return at an appointed time.

Quincannon moved deeper into the lamp-streaked gloom. Tiers of bunks lined both walls, each outfitted with nut-oil lamp, needle, pipe, bowl, and supply of *ah pin vin*. All of the bunks in the nearest tier were occupied. Most smokers lay still in various postures, carried to sticky slumber by the black stuff in their pipes. Only one here was a Caucasian, a man who lay propped on one elbow in the shadows, smiling fatuously as he held a lichee-nut shell of opium over the flame of his lamp. It made a spluttering, hissing noise as it cooked. Quincannon stepped close enough to determine that the man wasn't James Scarlett, then turned toward the far side of the den.

And there, finally, he found his man.

The young attorney lay motionless on one of the lower bunks at the rear, his lips shaping words as if he were chanting some song to himself. Had he been here the entire two days since his wife had last seen him? If he was in fact an expendable cog in the brewing trouble between the rival Hip Sing and Kwong Dock tongs, as their client, Andrea Scarlett, was afraid was the case, Chinatown was the worst possible place for him to hole up.

Quincannon shook him, slapped his beard-stubbled face. No response. Scarlett was a serious addict who regularly "swallowed a cloud and puffed out fog," as the Chinese said, and escaped for hours, sometimes days as in the present case, deep inside his pipe dreams — no doubt the reason he had sold his services, if not his soul, to the corrupt elements in the Hip Sing tong. An unlimited supply of opium was as great a lure to a hophead as the money he was paid to give legal aid to hatchet men and other Chinatown low-lifes.

"You're a blasted fool in more ways than one," Quincannon told the deaf ears. "It's a wonder you're not dead already."

He took a grip on the attorney's rumpled frock coat, hauled him around and off the bunk. There was no protest as he hoisted the slender body over his shoulder. The hanging opium smoke had begun to make him dizzy; he lurched a little as he groped toward the door with his burden. He was halfway there when his foot struck one of the cats darting through the gloom. It yowled and clawed at his leg, pitching him off balance. He reeled, cursing, against one of the bunks, dislodged a lamp from its edge; the glass chimney shattered on impact, splashing oil and wick onto the filthy floor matting.

The flame that sprouted was thin, shaky; the lack of oxygen in the room kept it from flaring high and spreading. Quincannon stamped out the meager fire, then strained over at the waist and reached down to right the lamp with his free hand. When he stood straight again, fighting off the dizziness, he heard someone giggle, someone else begin to sing in a low tone off-key. None of the pipers whose eyes were still open paid him the slightest attention. Neither did the smiling crone by the door as he staggered past her.

On the boardwalk outside, he paused to breathe deeply several times. The cold night air cleared his lungs and his head of the *ah pin vin* smoke, restored his equilibrium. He shifted Scarlett's inert weight on his shoulder. "Opium dens, a hophead lawyer, and a brewing tong war," he growled aloud. "Bah, what a muddle!"

It was his fault that Carpenter and Quincannon, Professional Detective Services, had agreed to take it on; Sabina had been less than enthusiastic. Ah, Sabina. Thinking of her immediately reminded him of the disturbing new development in her personal life that he'd only just learned of — her new suitor or beau or whatever the devil he was. Out with him on the town again tonight, no doubt, while her erstwhile and doting partner prowled the Chinatown alleys. Yes, and for all he knew, the fellow, one of the blasted society Montgomerys, was entertaining her this very minute in his digs, or perhaps they were together in her rooms on

Russian Hill. The unholy images this conjured up made him gnash his teeth.

He thrust the images away as Scarlett stirred, the cold night air having roused him somewhat from his stupor. The lawyer mumbled incoherent words, his body remaining limp in Quincannon's grasp.

Nearby, an old-fashioned gas street lamp cast a feeble puddle of light; farther along Ross Alley, toward Jackson Street where the hired hansom and driver waited, a few strings of paper lanterns and the glowing brazier of a lone sidewalk food seller opened small holes in the darkness. It was late enough, nearing ten o'clock, so that no pedestrians were abroad. Hardly any law-abiding Chinese ventured out at this hour. Nor had they in the past dozen years, since the rise of murderous tongs such as the Kwong Dock in the early eighties. The Quarter's nights belonged to the hop smokers and fantan gamblers, the slave-girl prostitutes ludicrously called "flower willows," and the *boo how doy,* the tongs' paid hatchet men.

Grumbling to himself, Quincannon lugged his semiconscious burden toward Jackson, his footsteps echoing on the rough cobbles. James Scarlett mumbled again, close enough to Quincannon's ear and with enough clarity for the words — and the low, fearful tone in which they were uttered — to be distinguishable.

"Fowler Alley," he said.

"What's that, my lad?"

A moan. And again, "Fowler Alley."

"Yes? What about it?"

Another moan, then something that might have been "Blue shadow."

"Not out here tonight," Quincannon muttered. "They're all black as the devil's fundament."

Ahead he saw the hansom's driver hunched fretfully on the seat of his rig, one hand holding the horse's reins and the other tucked inside his coat, doubtless resting on the handle of a revolver. Quincannon had had to pay him handsomely for this night's work — too handsomely to suit his thrifty Scots nature, even though he would see to it that his client, Mrs. James Scarlett, reimbursed him. If it had not been for the fact that highbinders almost never preyed on Caucasians, even a pile of greenbacks would not have been enough to bring the driver into Chinatown at midnight.

Twenty feet from the corner, Quincannon passed the lone food seller huddled over his brazier. He glanced at the man, noted the black coolie blouse with its drooping sleeves, the long queue, the head bent and shadow-hidden beneath a black slouch hat surmounted by a dark-colored topknot. He shifted his gaze to the hansom again, took two more steps —

Coolie food sellers don't wear slouch hats with topknots . . . they're one of the badges of the highbinder . . .

The sudden realization caused him to break stride and turn awkwardly under Scarlett's weight, his hand groping beneath his coat for the holstered Navy Colt. The Chinese assassin was already on his feet. From inside one sleeve he had drawn a long-barreled revolver; he aimed and fired before Quincannon could free his weapon.

The bullet struck the flaccid form of James Scarlett, made it jerk and slide free. The gunman fired twice more, loud reports in the close confines of the alley, but Quincannon was already falling sideways, his feet torn from under him by the attorney's toppling weight. Both slugs missed in the darkness, one whining in ricochet off the cobbles.

Quincannon struggled out from under the tangle of Scarlett's arms and legs. As he lurched to one knee he heard the retreating beat of the highbinder's footfalls. Heard, too, the rattle and slap of harness leather

31

and bit chains, the staccato pound of the horse's hooves as the hansom driver whipped out of harm's way. The gunman was a dim figure racing diagonally across Jackson. By the time Quincannon gained his feet, he had vanished into the black maw of Ragpickers' Alley.

Fury drove Quincannon into giving chase, even though he knew it was futile. Other narrow passages opened off Ragpickers' — Bull Run, Butchers' Alley with its clotted smells of poultry and fish. It was a maze made for the *boo how doy;* if he tried to navigate it in the dark, he was liable to become lost — or worse, leave himself wide open for ambush.

The wisdom of this slowed him to a halt ten rods into the lightless alleyway. He stood listening, breathing through his mouth. He could no longer hear the highbinder's footsteps now. Not that it mattered; even if they had been still audible, they would have been directionless here.

Quickly he returned to Jackson Street. The thoroughfare was empty, the driver and his rig long away. Ross Alley appeared deserted, too, but he could feel eyes peering at him from behind curtains and darkened glass. The hatchet man's brazier still burned; in its orange glow James Scarlett was a motionless hulk on the cobbles where he'd fallen.

Quincannon went to one knee beside him, probed with fingers that came away wet with blood. His words to Scarlett a short time ago echoed in his mind: *This is the last section of the city you should've ventured into this night. It's a wonder you're not dead already.* Well, the attorney was dead now, dead as the proverbial doornail. The first bullet had entered the middle of his back, shattering the spine and no doubt killing him instantly.

But three shots had been fired. Either the highbinder had been unsure of his marksmanship in the darkness, which was not generally the case with one of the *boo how doy* assassins, or Quincannon had been a target along with Scarlett. The second prospect both added to his anger and puzzled him. There was no sensible reason why the Kwong Dock tong, if in fact they were responsible for this outrage, would want him dead. For that matter, how could they have known he was on the hunt for the attorney tonight? Scarlett's wife had only just today retained the services of Carpenter and Quincannon, Professional Detective Services, and she would hardly have told anyone in the Quarter of her decision, as frightened as she was for his safety.

33

One thing was certain: An already tense situation had now become that much more volatile. A tong war between the Kwong Dock and the Hip Sing could erupt at any time. The theft of venerable Hip Sing president Bing Ah Kee's corpse four nights ago, assuming the Kwong Dock proved responsible for that as well, was fuel enough to fire hostilities. The murder of a Caucasian shyster and attempted murder of a Caucasian detective not only increased the likelihood of violence between the Chinese factions, but once the city's yellow journalists fanned the flames with their usual inflammatory zeal, there was the serious threat of retaliation by police raiders and mobs of Barbary Coast and Tar Flat toughs.

All of Chinatown, in short, might soon be a powder keg with a lighted fuse. And Quincannon, like it or not, was now caught up in it.

3
QUINCANNON

He used a police call box to report the whereabouts of the lawyer's corpse, left before the coppers arrived and coroner's wagon came to claim the body, and made his way directly to the Hall of Justice.

He disliked dealing with the city's constabulary; he'd had a number of run-ins with individuals of one rank or another who did not care to have their thunder stolen by a private investigator who was better at their jobs than they were. There was also the fact that police corruption had grown rampant in recent times. Not long ago there had been a departmental shake-up in which several officers and Police Clerk William E. Hall were discharged. Chief Crowley claimed all the bad apples had been removed and the barrel was now clean. Quincannon, however, remained more than a little skeptical.

But in this case, with James Scarlett murdered and a tong war a very real threat, he had no choice but to communicate what he knew and what he suspected. Not that he intended to work in consort with the police, even if Crowley would have allowed it. The murder of a man in his charge was not only a failure of professional responsibility but a personal affront, as was the possible attempt on his life tonight. He owed satisfaction to both his client and to himself, and that meant conducting an investigation of his own.

The Hall of Justice, an imposing gray stone pile at Kearney and Washington Streets, was within stampeding distance of the Chinese Quarter. Ten minutes after his arrival there, he was in the company of Chief Crowley, fortunately working late on this night, and two other ranking officers in the chief's private office.

One of the men he knew well enough, even grudgingly respected; this was Lieutenant William Price, head of the Chinatown "flying squad" that had been formed in an effort to control tong crime. He had mixed feelings about Crowley, and liked Sergeant Louis Gentry, Price's assistant, not at all. The feeling was mutual; Gentry made no bones about his distaste for flycops. But he seemed less contentious than usual tonight, evidently because of the gravity of the situation. The imminent danger of a bloody tong war was too great for personal feelings to interfere.

The three listened to Quincannon's tersely told tale without interruption and, for once, there were no hostile comments about his involvement in a criminal matter. The chief did demand the name of his client, and while he disliked revealing confidential information, the circumstances here dictated that he continue to be reasonably candid. Openly refusing to cooperate would be counterproductive.

"Scarlett's wife, eh?" Crowley said. He was an overweight sixty, florid and pompous. Politics was his game; his policeman's instincts were suspect, in Quincannon's view, a lacking which sometimes led him to rash judgment and action. "Hired you for what reason?"

"He hadn't been home in two nights, and naturally she was concerned and wanted him found."

"Afraid something might have happened to him?"

"Either that, or he'd gone off on a hop binge of longer than usual duration. Something had been bothering him lately, had him on edge and fearful."

"Something to do with the Hip Sing?"

"Mrs. Scarlett doesn't know."

"Or does know, and is keeping the knowledge to herself?"

"Doesn't know." She'd been vehement in her denial and Quincannon believed her. "She's aware of her husband's connection with the Hip Sing, but that's all. He never discussed his work with her, legal or otherwise."

"That fits with what we know about him," Price said. A big man, imposing in both bulk and thickly mustached countenance, he had a deserved reputation in Chinatown as the "American Terror," the result of raiding parties he'd led into the Quarter's more notorious dens of sin and corruption. "Closemouthed about his work for the Hip Sing."

Crowley said, "Then why was he targeted for a rubout?"

"Unreliable because of his opium addiction, maybe. Or else did something to displease the Hip Sing elders."

"You ask me, it wasn't a Hip Sing highbinder who shot him." This from Gentry, a bantam rooster of a man with the purple-veined cheeks of the habitual drinker. His gold-braided, gold-buttoned uniform, unlike those worn by his two superiors, was as immaculate as if he had only just come on duty. "Little Pete's behind this, sure as the devil. No one else in Chinatown would have the audacity to order the shooting of a white man."

"Why would Little Pete want to kill Scarlett?"

"For the same reason he ordered the Bing Ah Kee snatch. To start a tong war so he can take over the Hip Sing. That bloody devil already controls every other criminal tong in the Quarter."

This, Quincannon knew, was an exaggeration. Fong Ching, alias F. C. Peters, alias Little Pete, was a powerful man, no question — a curious mix of East and West, honest and crooked. He ran several successful businesses, participated in both Chinatown and city politics, and was cultured enough to write Chinese stage operas, yet he had for years ruled much of Chinatown's criminal activities with such guile that he had never been prosecuted. He had numerous enemies, however, and went about the Quarter outfitted in a steel-reinforced hat and chain-mail armor and accompanied by a trio of bodyguards. But other than his association with the Kwong Dock, his power was limited to a few sin-and-vice tongs. Most tongs, in particular the Chinese Six Companies, were law-abiding, self-governing, and benevolent.

Quincannon charged and fired his favorite briar and shook out the sulphur match before he said, "The Hip Sing is Pete's strongest rival. Granted, Mr. Price?"

"Yes. Granted."

"And he's not above starting a bloodbath in Chinatown to gain control of it," Gentry said. "He's a menace to white and yellow alike."

Price ran a forefinger across his bristly mustache. "Not so bad as that," he said. "Pete already controls most of the extortion and slave-girl rackets, and the Hip Sing is no threat to him there. Gambling is their primary enterprise, and under Bing Ah Kee there was never any serious trouble with the Kwong Dock or any of Pete's other outfits. That shouldn't change much under the new president, Mock Don Yuen."

Crowley said, "It could if that sneaky son of his, Mock Quan, ever takes over."

"Also granted."

"Pete's power-mad," Gentry said, continuing his argument. "He wants the whole of Chinatown crime in his pocket."

"Yes," Price agreed, "but he's wily, not crazy. He might have ordered the snatch of Bing's remains — though even the Hip Sing aren't convinced he's behind that business or war would have been declared already —

but I can't see him risking the public execution of a white man, not for any reason. He knows that's one thing Blind Chris won't stand for, and that it'd bring us down on him and his highbinders with a vengeance. He's too smart by half to take such a risk."

Quincannon tended to agree. Saloon-keeper Christopher A. "Blind Chris" Buckley was head of the city's powerful Democratic political machine and so notoriously corrupt that he was regularly vilified in the newspapers. It was common knowledge that Little Pete, among others, paid protection money to the "saloon boss" in order to remain in business. But as if to balance his corruption, Buckley was also noted for charity work and other civic contributions; he would never countenance an attack on a member of the white community. Honest officials such as Crowley, and Price and his Chinatown squad, were able to act independently of Buckley's criminal influence, but they needed clear-cut and indisputable evidence to do so without hazarding political consequences.

"Well, somebody took it," Gentry argued. "And Pete's the only man in that rathole of vice who'd dare."

"Not necessarily," Quincannon said. "Hidden forces at work, mayhap."

41

"Such as?"

He shrugged. "Merely a suggestion."

"Yeah, well, keep your suggestions to yourself. You don't know Pete or the Quarter like we do, flycop."

"No, Quincannon may be right," Price said. "I've had a feeling that there's more going on than meets the eye and ear in Chinatown these days. Yet we've learned nothing to corroborate it."

Quincannon said, "I take it you've had no word of what's become of Bing Ah Kee's remains?"

"None. There's no telling without a better understanding of the purpose of its theft."

The stubbornly churlish sergeant put his oar in again. "I say Pete's got the corpse in cold storage and intends to use it to start a war with the Hip Sing."

"If that's the case, why hasn't he produced it by now? Or demanded a ransom? It's been four days since the snatch."

Four days was in fact a long time without word of some sort. The body of old Bing Ah Kee, who had died of natural causes, had disappeared from the Four Families Temple near Hip Sing headquarters on Waverly Place. After a lavish funeral parade, it had been returned to the temple for one last night before it was scheduled for placement in storage to await passage to Bing's ancestral home in Canton for burial. The thieves had removed the corpse from its coffin and made off with it sometime during the early morning hours — a particularly bold deed considering the proximity of the temple to the Hip Sing Company. Yet they had managed it unseen and unheard, leaving no clues as to their identity.

Body snatching was uncommon but not unheard of in Chinatown. When such ghoulishness did occur, tong rivalry was almost always the motivation — a fact which supported Gentry's contention that the disappearance of Bing Ah Kee's husk was the work of Little Pete and the Kwong Dock. Yet stealing an enemy leader's bones without openly and immediately claiming responsibility was an odd way of warmongering . . . unless the delay was a deliberate attempt to ratchet up tensions and make open warfare inevitable.

But then, why hadn't the usual gambit of instigating one or more assassinations of key figures in the rival tong been employed? And why would Little Pete, if he was the ringleader, send one of his highbinders to murder a white attorney instead?

"Well, in any case I don't like the way the wind is blowing over there," the chief said.

"This damned shooting tonight is bound to have dire consequences. The *boo how doy* have always left Caucasians strictly alone. You all know that. Scarlett's murder sets a deadly precedent."

"Exactly," Gentry said. "We can't afford to stand by and do nothing about it. Once the newshounds get hold of Scarlett's murder, they'll whip the public up to a froth. If we don't act soon, we're likely to have vigilante trouble to contend with, too."

"We damned well can't have that," Crowley said. "What do you suggest, Sergeant?"

"Smash Little Pete and his gang before more innocent citizens are killed."

"James Scarlett was hardly innocent," Price reminded him. "And we have no knowledge yet of why he was murdered, much less evidence that it was Pete who ordered it."

"Then let's go find some." Gentry had lighted a cheap long nine cigar; he waved it for emphasis. "By God, the only way to ensure public safety is to send the flying squad out to Pete's shoe factory and the Kwong Dock headquarters. Axes, hammers, and pistols will write his and his highbinders' epitaphs in a hurry."

"Not yet," Price said, still the voice of reason.

"Why not?"

"For one thing, Pete's too clever to leave evidence lying around for us to find."

"He is, maybe, but his henchmen may not be."

Price ignored this. "And for another," he said, "a premature raid is liable to have the opposite effect, especially if Pete turns out to be innocent. Cause widespread bloodshed instead of preventing it. And bring the wrath of Blind Chris and his machine down on our heads." He appealed to the chief. "Don't you agree, sir?"

Crowley was silent. He seemed to be considering the dubious wisdom of Gentry's suggestion.

Price realized it, too. "I strongly advise against a show of force at this time." Then, for emphasis, he repeated, *"Strongly."*

The chief made up his mind — the correct decision, to Quincannon's way of thinking. "You're right, Will," he said. "We'll hold off for the time being, see how the wind blows."

Gentry forbore further argument, though with obvious reluctance. He gave a dissatisfied nod, saluted, and left the office.

When the door closed behind him, Quincannon said to Price, "What do you know of Fowler Alley, Lieutenant?"

"Fowler Alley? Why do you ask that?"

"Scarlett mumbled the name after I carried him out of the opium resort. I wonder if it might have significance."

"I can't imagine how. Little Pete operates his little empire from his shoe factory in Bartlett Alley, near the Kwong Dock Company. There are no tong headquarters in Fowler Alley, and no known illegal activity other than a fantan parlor or two."

"Are any of the businesses there run by Pete?"

"Not to my knowledge. I'll look into it."

Quincannon nodded, thinking, *Not before I do, by Godfrey.* He got to his feet. "I'll be going now, gentlemen. My client has to be told of her husband's death."

Crowley said, "I can dispatch a man to do that —"

"No, the chore is mine." The mere thought of it knotted Quincannon's insides, but he was not a man to shirk his duty where a client was concerned. Especially not when the slaying victim had been in his care at the time of the attack. But that was not the only reason. If Andrea Scarlett did after all possess even a scrap of information germane to her husband's murder, he wanted to know what it was before the police did.

The chief shrugged and waved a dismissive

46

hand. "You'll be notified if you're needed again. Meanwhile, you'll do well to remember that you have no official standing in this matter. Do I make myself clear?"

Quincannon said, "Perfectly," between his teeth, and took his leave.

The law offices of James Scarlett were on the southern fringe of Chinatown, less than half a mile from the Hall of Justice. For this reason, Quincannon made that his first stop. He had briefly visited the old, two-story wooden building earlier in the day, after Andrea Scarlett had departed the agency and before venturing into Chinatown. The place had been dark and locked up tight then; the same was true when he arrived there a few minutes before midnight.

He paid the hansom driver at the corner, walked back through heavy shadows to the entranceway. Pondering the while, as he had in the cab, about the sinister incident in Ross Alley.

Why had the hatchet man waited in ambush as he had? If he'd known Scarlett was in the Cellar of Dreams, why not just enter and dispose of him there? Witnesses were never a worry to the *boo how doy.* Could he, Quincannon, have been followed on his rounds of the opium resorts? No. Always

47

sensitive to his surroundings, particularly in such places as Chinatown after dark, he was sure that he hadn't been tailed.

Then there was the fact that the assassin had fired three shots, the last two of which had come perilously close to sending Quincannon to join *his* ancestors. Wildly hurried shooting caused by darkness? Or, as unlikely as it might seem, could he also have been a target? There was something about the shooter that fretted him, too, something he could not quite put his finger on.

The whole business smacked of hidden motives, to be sure. And hidden dangers. He did not like to be made a pawn in any piece of intrigue for any reason. He disliked it almost as much as being shot at, intentionally or otherwise, and failing at a job he had been retained to do. He meant to get to the bottom of it, with or without official sanction.

Few door latches had ever withstood his ministrations with lock picks and skeleton keys, and the one on the entrance to James Scarlett's building was no exception. Another lawyer occupied the downstairs rooms; Quincannon climbed a creaky staircase to the second floor. He had no need to use quasi-legal means to gain access here: the pebbled glass door imprinted with the words J. H. SCARLETT, ATTORNEY-AT-LAW was not locked. This puzzled him somewhat, though not for long.

Inside, he struck a lucifer, found and lighted the gas — the building was too old and shabby to have been wired for electricity. Its pale glow showed him an anteroom containing two desks whose bare surfaces indicated that they might never have been used. According to Andrea Scarlett, her husband had intended to move to more fashionable downtown offices, and to hire both a law clerk and a secretary, but the combination of his work for the Hip Sing and his increasingly powerful opium addiction had kept him rooted here.

Quincannon proceeded through a doorway into Scarlett's private sanctum. His first impression was that the lawyer had been a remarkably untidy individual. A few seconds later he revised this opinion; the office had been searched in what appeared to be a hurried and careless fashion. Papers littered the top of a large oak desk, the floor around it and the floor before a bank of wooden file cases. Two of the file drawers were partly open, manila folders yanked half out and askew inside. A wastebasket behind the desk had been overturned and its contents strewn about. A shelf of dusty law books showed signs of having been pawed through as well.

The work of a highbinder? Possibly, though the search struck him as a a good deal less destructive than what he was used to seeing from henchmen of any race. Done, then, by someone who wanted it to look like one of the *boo how doy* was responsible?

The smell of must and mildew wrinkled his nostrils as he crossed to the desk, giving him to wonder just how much time Scarlett had spent in these premises in recent weeks. The office wanted a good airing, if not a match to purge it completely. Scowling, he sifted through the papers on and below the desk.

There were several files concerning Scarlett's recent clients, almost all of whom were Hip Sing Chinese he had defended in court, with surprising success, on gambling and other criminal charges. One bore a label with a familiar name: Mock Don Yuen, the successor to Bing Ah Kee as head of the tong. Just what Scarlett had been doing on behalf of Mock Don Yuen was unclear. The scant file contained only a pair of legal briefs that concerned gambling-related court cases in which Mock Don Yuen had been called upon to testify, and a two-page document composed entirely of Chinese characters. Written by the tong leader, perhaps? In any event it must have had something to do with him, else it wouldn't have been in his file. Quincannon removed the document and folded it into his pocket.

The desk drawers yielded nothing of interest, and the slim accumulation of briefs, letters, and invoices in the file drawers was likewise uninformative. None contained any direct reference to either the Hip Sing or Kwong Dock tongs, or to Fong Ching under his own name or any of his known aliases.

The only interesting thing about the late Mr. Scarlett's office, other than the document in Mock Don Yuen's file, was the state in which Quincannon had found it. What had the previous intruder been searching for? And whatever it was, had he left with what he'd come after?

The Scarletts' home address, in the polyglot neighborhood known as Cow Hollow, turned out to be a three-story wood-and-brick apartment building with an ornate façade. They had lived there only a short while, Andrea Scarlett had said, having moved from "a less comfortable" residence at her insistence once the Hip Sing arrangement had been made.

The windows facing the street in their third-floor apartment were all dark. But this

51

proved not to be because Mrs. Scarlett had retired for the night. Quincannon knocked several times, loud enough to rouse even the heaviest sleeper. Not at home at this hour?

The second of his skeleton keys opened the locked door. A hasty search revealed no sign of her. Each of the four large rooms was empty and showed no signs of disturbance.

The apartment was chilly, long unheated either by gas or coal fire in the living room fireplace. The sheets on the carelessly made four-poster bed were likewise cold. Nothing in the kitchen indicated that a meal had been prepared or eaten recently. If Andrea Scarlett had been home since her visit to the agency offices late that afternoon, it had been only briefly.

Quincannon resisted the urge to conduct a more thorough search, stepped out, and relocked the door. Well past midnight now. Where was his client at this hour? Hiding out somewhere, unable to bear remaining alone in her home? Possibly. She had been most concerned about her husband during the morning's interview, but the fact that she had seen someone lurking about the premises the night before had made her afraid for herself as well.

Her absence was worrisome, in any event. Very.

In his rooms on Leavenworth, Quincannon lay sleepless and brooding for much of what remained of the night. Bing Ah Kee's missing corpse, Scarlett's murder and the attempt on his own life, the search of the lawyer's offices, Little Pete, the Kwong Dock, the Hip Sing, the potential actions of Price and Gentry and the Chinatown flying squad. Andrea Scarlett, suddenly a widow and certain to be an understandably upset client. And Sabina and her new swain.

It was the Sabina question that plagued him most into the wee hours. The others would be resolved, one way or another, in relatively short order. But Sabina's involvement with this Montgomery gent was a mystery — one he'd only just learned about by accident, and that she steadfastly refused to discuss — that could have long-reaching implications and might not be solvable at all, depending on the seriousness of her interest in Montgomery and his in her. If it was merely an interlude, an innocent infatuation, then there was no cause for concern. Ah, but if it was serious to the point of intimacy, perhaps even engagement and marriage . . .

Thunder and blazes! Quincannon's heart was hard enough when it came to the female sex, but not indestructible. His partner, the object of his unrequited desire, was the one woman who could break it.

4
QUINCANNON

On his way down Market Street from his cable car stop on Wednesday morning, Quincannon paused at a news vendor's stand to buy copies of the *Chronicle* and the *Morning Call.* He opened the former first as he walked. As he'd feared, the newshounds had gotten wind of the previous night's shooting. The murder of a white man in Chinatown even provoked outrage against the "heathen Chinee" in the city's largest and perhaps most conservative sheet, the *Chronicle.* Its editorial staff, like that of the *Call,* ballyhooed the incident with front-page headlines.

PROMINENT ATTORNEY
SLAIN IN CHINATOWN
James Scarlett Gunned Down
in Ross Alley
Police Fear Threat of Tong War

Faugh. Prominent attorney, my hindquarters,
Quincannon thought. Typical journalistic
twaddle. Why should the sudden demise of
an opium-addicted shyster elevate him to a
position of prominence in the legal community? If every lawyer in San Francisco
guilty of corrupt or dubious practices was
suddenly murdered, and there were a great
many who deserved that fate, they would
no doubt be lionized in the press as brilliant
and virtuous defenders of the law.

Quincannon read the accompanying story
as he walked, then the one in the *Call.* Both
were about as he'd expected, more speculation than fact in linking Scarlett's murder
to the theft of Bing Ah Kee's corpse four
nights previous and the general state of
unrest in the Quarter. On the positive side,
his name was not mentioned and the writing was far more restrained than what was
sure to appear in the afternoon rags. Homer
Keeps, the *Evening Bulletin*'s muckraking
crime reporter, would be sure to use the
death of a white man at the hands of a highbinder to stir up more virulent hatred of the
Chinese among the populations of Tar Flat
and the Barbary Coast, where such senti-
ments ran strongest. And if one of the less
scrupulous coppers at the Hall of Justice
leaked Quincannon's name for a price,

56

Keeps would gleefully insinuate that he was either directly or indirectly responsible.

The reporter had had it in for him since his days as a Secret Service operative and the tragic incident in Virginia City, Nevada, when a stray bullet from Quincannon's pistol during a battle with a gang of counterfeiters had taken the life of an innocent woman bystander and her unborn child. As if his guilt hadn't been crippling enough, Keeps and others of his ilk had made it worse by mercilessly condemning him in print. His subsequent plunge into drunkenness would have cost him his job if it hadn't been for the charity of Mr. Boggs, head of the Service's San Francisco field office, and perhaps then doomed him to permanent ruin. It was only after coincidentally meeting Sabina, while they were both working undercover on separate cases in Idaho, that he'd retaken command of his life and become the sober detective he was today. Keeps, however, had no forgiveness in his soul, and continued to hound him whenever the opportunity presented itself.

Sabina was already at her desk when he entered the offices of Carpenter and Quincannon, Professional Detective Services, a few minutes later. She invariably arrived earlier than he did, to tidy the office as well as to begin her daily activities. Much of the paperwork — reports, invoices, payment of bills — was her responsibility by choice. He was organized when it came to work on a specific case, disorganized where routine business matters were concerned. It was paperwork she was attending to this morning when he entered.

The look of her had two distinct effects on him. The first was an unpleasant feeling that his fears of the night before might be justified, for she seemed distracted, as if something were weighing on her mind — something to do with that fop Carson Montgomery. Had she succumbed to his advances and was having second thoughts about such a dalliance? Had he — God forbid — proposed to her in or out of bed and was she considering whether or not to accept?

The other, contradictory feeling was a surge of jealousy-fueled desire. Such an intelligent, skillful, and good-hearted woman. And such a desirable one, her glossy black hair piled high on her head and fastened with her favorite jeweled barrette, her ample bosom made even more prominent by the tight bodice of her shirtwaist. The two feelings combined to stoke the wicked side of his imagination, bring into his mind's eye a slightly feverish image of that fine figure divested of its skirt and jacket, shirtwaist and lacy undergarments, submitting to the leering gaze of that society coxcomb Montgomery . . .

She narrowed her eyes at him as he shed his derby and Chesterfield and crossed to his desk. "Before we get down to business," she said, "I'll thank you to put my clothes back on."

"Eh?" Sudden warmth crept out of Quincannon's collar. "Sabina! Surely you don't think that I —"

"I don't think it, I know it. I know you, John Quincannon, far better than you think I do."

He said defensively, "Perhaps, though you often mistake my motives."

"I doubt that. Was your sleepless night the result of rewarding that lascivious mind of yours?"

"How did you know I spent a sleepless night —"

"Bloodshot eyes in saggy pouches. If I didn't know better, I'd think you had forsaken your temperance pledge with whatever wench you were canoodling with."

"I was not canoodling with anyone last night." It was on the tip of Quincannon's tongue to ask her the same question; he managed to bite it off just in time. He was not supposed to be aware that she was keeping company with the socially prominent Carson Montgomery. She hadn't said a word to him about the man, of course, her steadfast position as always being that the details of her private life were not to be shared. If he were to ask pointed questions or to speak Montgomery's name, it would cause immediate friction. And gain him no knowledge of the extent of their relationship. She would simply tell him to mind his own business and immediately change the subject.

No, the time had not yet come to let her know that he was aware of her attachment to Carson Montgomery. Might never come, if his jealous imaginings turned out to be unfounded. He consoled himself with the thought that he'd misinterpreted her distracted look, that something that had little or nothing to do with Montgomery was the cause of it. Still, the possibility that she had granted the confounded socialite her favors, or was about to do so, would continue to plague him until he found out the exact nature of their relationship.

And he *would* find out, not by resorting to spying but by judicious detective work when time permitted. Theodore Bonesall, the banker and former client from whom he'd learned of Sabina dining tête-à-tête with her new beau on at least two recent evenings, was only one of many well-placed acquaintances he could call on for the necessary information . . .

"What's the matter, John?"

"Eh? Matter?"

"Your expression. You look as though you're having a gastric attack."

Gastric attack. Faugh! He couldn't help a wry grimace as he said, "My innards are fine, thank you."

"Well, I'm glad to hear it. If that expression is because I offended you with my canoodling remark, I apologize. It was inappropriate, given our agreement to limit our daily intercourse to professional matters only."

The word "intercourse" caused him to grimace again, somewhat wistfully this time, though he managed to turn his head so that Sabina was not witness to it. He sighed inaudibly as he sat at his desk. Love, especially unrequited love, was not only a difficult proposition, it was a confounded nuisance.

He produced and began to charge his briar, preparatory to giving Sabina a full dramatic report of the previous night's events. But just as he was about to speak, Mr. Alexander Graham Bell's invention filled the office with a sudden clamoring.

Quincannon glowered at the telephone, which was closest to Sabina's desk. She lifted the receiver in the middle of a second jangle. Static crackled audibly from the line, enough interference, judging from her end of the conversation, to make communication with the calling party, evidently a woman named Blankford or Branchford, difficult. He gave his attention to his small stack of morning mail. Checks were what he was looking for; bills and solicitations all that he found.

When the call ended, Sabina said, "It appears we have a new client, or at least the strong prospect of one. Mrs. Harriet Blanchford, Ruben Blanchford's widow."

"Ruben Blanchford? Ah!" Quincannon's interest perked. "The financier. Made a fortune from the Comstock Lode along with Hearst, William Sharon, and Alvinza Hayward."

"Yes, and spent his later years engaged in philanthropic enterprises. He died a few days ago of a heart ailment."

"Worth several millions, as I recall."

"Evidently. Quite a pleasant gentleman, too."

"That sounds as though you knew him."

"Hardly. I happen to have met him at a reception at the Palace Hotel a year or so ago."

"Reception? I don't recall you mentioning that before. Were you there in conjunction with a case?"

"No."

"As an invited guest? Or in the company of one?"

"That's neither here nor there." Sabina's narrow-eyed look chastised him for prying into her personal life again. Blast her passion for privacy! "Don't you want to know the reason for Mrs. Blanchford's call?"

"Naturally. What's her trouble?"

"Well, I'm not quite sure. Something about a kidnapping."

"Oh? Who has been abducted?"

"Her husband, I thought she said, but that's hardly possible. As usual with the Telephone Exchange, the connection was poor. I managed to make an appointment with her at her home at one-thirty."

A kidnapping, eh? That sort of major crime usually involved considerable investigative time and effort. Visions of a handsome fee danced in Quincannon's head, overshadowing the unpleasant ones involving Sabina and Carson Montgomery.

He said, "Of course we'll do all we can to give the poor woman whatever help she needs."

"Of course. Especially since the poor woman is anything but poor."

Quincannon forbore comment on this. Instead he said, "Now would you like to know what I was actually doing all of last night?"

"If it involves business, I would."

"It does. Hunting for James Scarlett, as promised to his wife."

"And did you find him?"

"Oh, I found him well enough. As you'd know if you'd seen the morning newspapers."

"The newspapers? That sounds ominous. What happened, John?"

"He was shot to death in Chinatown while in my charge," Quincannon said, and added after a deliberate pause, "It was only by the narrowest of margins that I escaped the same fate."

One of Sabina's fine dark eyebrows lifted and the corners of her mouth tightened. "Who was responsible?"

"A hatchet man posing as a food seller."

He went on to describe in detail the events in Ross Alley and his activities afterward, including the things that bothered him

64

about the incident and the speculations he'd shared with the three ranking police officers. When he finished, the smooth skin of Sabina's forehead and around her generous mouth bore lines of concern.

"Bad business," she said. "And bad for business. Not that you're to be blamed, of course."

"No, but others will surely blame me. The only way to undo the damage is for me to find out who ordered the murder and why, before any more blood is shed and before Horace Keeps and his ilk crucify me in print."

"Us to find out, you mean."

"Us," he agreed. "Though you'd be well advised not to venture into Chinatown."

"I have no intention of it. Though I suppose you do."

"It's where the truth lies."

"And Fowler Alley?" Sabina asked. "What do you suppose that has to do with Scarlett's death?"

"Perhaps nothing, if his mutterings were part of a hop dream."

"You said he sounded frightened when he spoke the name. Opium dreams are seldom nightmares. Men and women use the drug to escape from nightmares, real or imaginary."

65

"True."

"Then his mention of Fowler Alley has some significance, wouldn't you say? 'Blue shadow' as well."

"Possibly," Quincannon allowed. "Though I can't be positive of the latter phrase. I may have misheard it."

"Was it spoken in the same fearful tone?"

He cudgeled his memory. "I can't be certain."

"If it was 'blue shadow,' you've no idea what it might mean?"

"None."

"Our client may have," Sabina said. "If she's home or to be found elsewhere today."

"Will you see if you can locate her before you keep your appointment with Mrs. Blanchford?"

Sabina hesitated. "I had another matter I intended to pursue . . . but it can wait. The Scarlett case takes precedence. Yes, I'll try to find her."

"Good. And if you talk to her, ask her where she was last night. A woman is more apt to confide in another member of her sex."

"I will."

"You might also ask her if she has any idea where her husband might have kept sensitive material pertaining to his Hip Sing

66

activities, other than in his office files. Whoever searched the office before I did may not have found what he was after."

"You don't think the search was made by the highbinder who shot Scarlett?"

"It seems unlikely."

"Has it occurred to you that Mrs. Scarlett may have done it? To look for evidence of her husband's criminal activities, perhaps destroy it?"

"It has. But the search was made either before or shortly after he was murdered. I see no way she could have known of the shooting before I made my search last night, and it doesn't seem likely she would have invaded his office while believing him to be alive. It would have served no purpose."

"True. Then who do you suppose is responsible, if not a highbinder or our client? Whoever is behind Scarlett's murder?"

"Likely. Whoever in Chinatown that may be."

"Is there anything you can remember about the gunman that might help identify his tong affiliation?"

Quincannon puffed up a great cloud of tobacco smoke, scratched irritably at his freebooter's whiskers. "No, confound it. It was too dark and his hat was pulled too low for a clear squint at his face. Average size, average height. Black coolie clothing. Dark-colored topknot on his hat of the sort high-binders wear."

"Did he say anything before he began shooting?"

"Not a word." Quincannon stood and went to don his Chesterfield and clamp his derby on his head, squarely, the way he always wore it when he was about to embark on a mission. "Enough talk. It's action I crave and action I'll have."

"Not of the sort you had last night, I hope," Sabina said.

"If there's to be any more shooting," he vowed, "it will be my finger on the trigger and a highbinder on the receiving end of the bullet."

5
SABINA

She hadn't told John about the bughouse Sherlock Holmes's evident interest in Carson Montgomery for three reasons. The first was that it would have upset him unnecessarily, considering how he felt about the poseur. The second: She wasn't completely positive that the Englishman had been following Carson last night, and even if she had been, she needed to know the reason why before she considered taking John into her confidence. The third: her embryonic relationship with Carson was too personal and too uncertain, and any mention of it to John was sure to bring down an avalanche of disapproval. There were moments when she thought of him as an overprotective father, rather than a professional associate and wistful suitor.

Still, keeping silent on the matter gave her an odd sense of disloyalty to him. Her personal life was her own, as was his, and that was as it should be, but from the inception of their partnership they had been completely candid with each other on business matters. She really didn't like keeping secrets from him.

Nonetheless, Holmes's inexplicable actions and Carson's apparent secretiveness continued to prey on her mind. Her original intention this morning had been to consult with those among the agency's informants who might be able to discover where the fake Sherlock could be presently found, if not what he was up to, as well as those who had occasion to deal with the city's upper classes and might have knowledge of anything disturbing in Carson's past. Cousin Callie would have been the most likely person to see first, but Callie was a staunch admirer of Carson and would have been horrified to hear that Sabina had any doubts that he was a social and personal paragon. Better that she should conduct her inquiries through professional channels.

But seeing informants would have to wait until later. The Scarlett case, now that the attorney had been slain and John nearly so, was of much greater importance. And there was the afternoon appointment with Harriet Blanchford to be considered as well. So when she left the agency, she proceeded directly to the Scarletts' home at the edge of Cow Hollow.

The neighborhood was an unusual one, even for San Francisco. Irrigated by several freshwater creeks, it had been ideal grazing land where many dairies and vegetable farms had been established in earlier times. By the late eighties, tanneries, sausage factories, and slaughterhouses began moving into the area, and for a time there had been numerous episodes of hoodlumism. Now it was slowly becoming gentrified. A number of prominent individuals had moved there, into new two- and three-story apartment buildings that overshadowed their more plebeian neighbors.

The Scarletts' address was one of those new buildings, in the lower section of the Hollow overlooking what once had been a lake, now filled in, called "Washerwoman's Lagoon." Sabina was about to ring the bell in the vestibule for the third-floor apartment when, keen-eyed as always, she noticed a small hole in the wall next to the front door. It was waist high, so that she had to stoop to examine it.

It was a bullet hole, with the lead pellet still embedded in the wood. And judging from the look of its splintered edges, it had been recently made.

She entered and quickly climbed the stairs to the Scarlett apartment on the third floor. Two twists on the doorbell key and two raps on the panel produced no response. The door was locked, as John had apparently left it last night. He'd been inside and found nothing, so there was no need for her to make use of her own limited lock-picking skills.

She descended to the second floor. No one answered her summons at that apartment, either. But when she rang the bell to the first-floor unit, the door opened on a chain, and a rather amazing eye, kohl-rimmed so that it resembled a raccoon's, peered out at her.

"Yes? What is it?" The woman's voice was a rusty contralto.

"I'm looking for one of your neighbors, Mrs. Andrea Scarlett."

"You a friend of hers?"

Apparently the woman hadn't yet heard the news of James Scarlett's murder. Sabina had one of her cards ready; she held it up for the eye to scrutinize. It widened, narrowed, widened again. "Well, my goodness! A detective! A *woman* detective!"

To forestall anything further in that vein, Sabina asked, "Have you seen Mrs. Scarlett in the past twenty-four hours?"

"Last evening about eight-thirty. That why you're here?"

"What happened at eight-thirty?"

There was a pause. Then the eye disappeared, the chain rattled, and the door popped open to reveal the rest of the woman's middle-aged face. It was as amazing as the black-ringed eye. Pale blond hair pulled to the top of her head, from where it frizzled down like champagne from a fountain. Bright orange rouge on both cheeks and smeared over a thick-lipped mouth. Around her neck was a multi-colored feather boa, and in one hand she held the gaudiest, ugliest hat Sabina had ever seen.

Her expression must have betrayed her surprise, for the woman said, "Don't mind the way I look, honey. I'm a performer at the Hermann's Gaiety. Me and some other girls do a comic singing act . . . matinees this week. I was just about to leave for the theatre."

"I see."

"Astrid Allegra's my stage name. My husband's a famous magician, the Great Santini, you probably heard of him."

"No, I'm sorry, I haven't. About last night, Mrs. Santini —"

"Jones. Agnes Jones. Santini, that's Hiram's stage name."

"About last evening. What happened?"

The orange-rouged lips thinned. "Some damn hoodlum fired off a gun right out front, that's what happened. Came within a whisper of hitting poor Mrs. Scarlett. Scared her half to death."

Eight-thirty last evening. It had been nearly midnight when John came; he hadn't mentioned the bullet hole, so he must have missed seeing it in the darkness.

Sabina asked, "Did you witness the shooting?"

"No. I heard the report and ran out just as she came in."

"Did she see who fired the shot?"

"Didn't say so if she did. Too shaken up to say much of anything, poor lamb."

"What happened then?"

"Well, I tried to coax her to come in for some, ah, tea to settle herself down, but she refused. Didn't go upstairs to her rooms, either. Just said, 'I can't stay here,' and ran out the back way. Never came back, far as I know."

"So you have no idea where she went?"

"Maybe to find her husband. If she didn't find him, he must've been real surprised when he got home and she wasn't there."

"She may also have gone to be with a friend," Sabina said. "Do you know any of her intimates?"

The woman considered, nibbling at her rouged upper lip. "Well, I don't know her all that well. But we got to passing the time of day once, just after her and her husband moved in, and found out we have a bit in common. She was never a performer, but before she married Mr. Scarlett she worked as a seamstress sewing costumes at the Bella Union. It was a friend of hers, the wardrobe mistress, who got her the job there, she said."

"Do you remember the friend's name?"

"Just her given name — Delilah. Unusual, that's why I remember it. Girlhood chums, as I recall."

It seemed a tenuous lead, but any at this point was worth pursuing. Sabina thanked Astrid Allegra née Agnes Jones, wished her and the Great Santini well in their professional careers, and took her leave.

The Bella Union, on the north side of Washington Street off Portsmouth Square, was the city's most popular purveyor of variety, minstrel, and burlesque shows. Originally, Sabina had been told, it had been a gambling saloon, then a melodeon, and now, in addition to its main attractions, it housed both a small waxworks and a penny arcade. Although it was located in the Barbary Coast, it catered to all strata of local society and featured all manner of high and low performances. The highest: Lotta Crabtree entertaining during the Gold Rush era with such skill and "incredible innocence," as pundits of the day had termed it, that wealthy miners were said to have tossed gold nuggets at her feet. The lowest: a famously ludicrous attempt to portray the male lead in *Romeo and Juliet* by Oofty Goofty — a local character who had once billed himself as "The Wild Man of Borneo" by covering his body with a mixture of tar and horsehair and fiercely yelling "Oofty goofty!" while eating raw meat in a locked cage in a Market Street sideshow.

A hansom delivered Sabina to the Bella Union shortly before eleven-thirty. The two-story building had a brick façade strung with electric lights that glittered with a star-like effect after dark, an advertising decoration that had become fashionable at the better gaiety palaces. Its main entrance was closed at this hour. An alleyway along one side led to the stage door at the rear, which was presided over, just inside, by an elderly twig of a man wearing flowered galluses and a clashing green eyeshade. Despite his age, his memory for faces was obviously keen —

clearly one of the reasons, if not the primary one, that he had been given his job.

"Help you, miss?" he asked in crisp tones.

Sabina favored him with her brightest smile. "I'd like to see Delilah if she's here."

"Delilah? You mean Miz Brown, the wardrobe mistress?"

"Yes, that's right."

"She expecting you?"

"No, but it's important that I speak with her."

"What about?"

"A mutual friend. My name is Sabina Carpenter."

She handed him one of her cards, which he frowned over and which made him even more wary and not a little scornful. "Woman detective. What's the world coming to?"

Sabina was used to this kind of reaction from the general male population. At one time it had made her furious and more often than not she had responded with a tart comment or two, but she had learned to control herself; now it merely rankled. Times, after all, were changing. Too slowly to suit her, but changing nonetheless. Women had been granted the right to vote in New Zealand, Sweden, and Finland, and women's suffrage organizations were gaining popularity in eastern portions of the

United States. It was only a matter of time until members of her sex finally achieved at least a measure of the equality they were entitled to. Until then, she would have to continue to suffer, as stoically as possible, the narrow-minded attitudes of men such as this one.

She managed to hold most of her smile in place as she said, "Would you please deliver my card and my message to Delilah," making it a firm statement rather than a question.

He made grumbling noises, but didn't decline or argue. He got slowly to his feet, said, "Wait here, missus," and hobbled away into the depths of the theatre's backstage area.

Not more than two minutes had elapsed when he returned with a slender young woman whose dark hair was bound up in a snood. The woman was clearly nervous; her smile wobbled a bit and she plucked at a thimble covering the tip of one forefinger as she approached. Sabina's demeanor seemed to reassure her. Even before she spoke, Sabina knew that Agnes Jones's lead had proven not to be tenuous after all, for there was relief as well as anxiety in Delilah Brown's steady gaze.

"I'm so glad you've come, Mrs. Carpenter.

Our . . . mutual friend will be glad to see you, too. She told me so much about you."

"Is she here?"

"No." Delilah glanced at the old man, who had sat down again and was watching them. "Shall we talk outside? I could do with a breath of fresh air."

When they were alone together in the alley, Sabina asked, "You do know where I can find Andrea Scarlett?"

"Oh, yes. But how did you know to come to me?"

"A stroke of good fortune. Where is she?"

"At my rooming house, not far from here. Seven forty-two Pine Street, second floor front."

"She spent the night with you?"

"Yes. She was afraid to go to the police." Delilah's hands continued to fret against each other, continually removing and replacing the thimble. "Someone . . . last night someone tried to murder her, too."

"So I understand. She knows about her husband, then?"

"From the newspapers this morning. Poor Andrea, she's terribly upset and frightened. She wants desperately to see you, but she couldn't bring herself to go out into the streets again even in daylight."

"Does anyone else know she's there?"

"No, I'm sure not. She's welcome to stay
—"

"That won't be necessary. I'll make arrangements for her safety and protection."

"She'll be so relieved." Then, with sudden vehemence, "Andrea may be sorry James is dead, but I'm not. I hope he roasts in the fires of hell for all he put her through."

The overnight change in Andrea Scarlett was shocking. Yesterday at the agency she had been neatly coiffed and stylishly dressed, and despite her fears, in rigid control of her emotions. Today, she wore a borrowed housecoat and a look of naked terror. She sat hugging herself in one of the chairs in Delilah Brown's parlor, her narrow, high-cheekboned face the color of whey, her auburn hair uncombed and lusterless, her eyes red-rimmed from weeping, lack of sleep, or a combination of both. But she was less distraught now than she had been when Sabina first arrived, Sabina's calming influence having shored up her courage.

"No, Mrs. Carpenter," she said, "I didn't have a clear look at the man who tried to kill me last night. He was waiting in shadows across from the entrance when I returned from an errand. I managed to duck inside

80

before he could fire again and he ran off into the darkness. All I can tell you is that he was short and wore white man's clothing."

"What sort of clothing?"

"A hat and a dark-colored suit."

"Type of hat?"

"I'm not sure. I think it had a broad brim pulled down low."

"Such as the slouch type Chinese wear?"

"No, not like that." Andrea Scarlett hugged herself more tightly. "But he *must* have been Chinese. It was one of those dreadful highbinders who shot James, wasn't it? That's what the newspapers said . . ."

"One dressed as a food seller outside the opium resort, yes."

There was a little silence. When the woman spoke again, her tone was bitter. "James and his opium. James and his greed and his lust."

"Lust, Mrs. Scarlett?"

"For Chinese women. I didn't say anything about that to you and Mr. Quincannon yesterday because I was too ashamed."

More ashamed of her husband's infidelity than of his drug addiction. People could be perplexingly and irritatingly inconsistent.

"Was there any woman in particular?"

Sabina asked.

"Yes. One named Dongmei."

"Who is she?"

"A courtesan, I suppose . . . that's the polite term. She introduced James to opium."

"You're sure of that?"

"Fairly sure."

"Before or after he became involved with the Hip Sing?"

"Before, I think. Not long before."

"How do you know her name?"

"He spoke it in his sleep, more than once. Admitted his affair with her when I confronted him."

"Why didn't you tell us about Dongmei yesterday? Didn't you think your husband might have been with her instead of in an opium resort?"

"No. James never spent the night with her or any of his other women. Opium was his only true love."

"Yet despite his vices, you stayed with him. Why?"

Andrea Scarlett released a stuttery breath. "I've asked myself that question dozens of times. The truth is, I don't know why. I stopped loving James long before he became involved with the Hip Sing. The money he made, the better life for us it provided . . .

that had something to do with it, I won't deny that. So did the fact that he needed me. In spite of his other women, in spite of his addiction, he *needed* me . . ."

Sabina made no comment. She had encountered many women who felt as Mrs. Scarlett did toward a philandering husband, and while she didn't blame them for their weakness, neither did she condone it. She herself had too much pride, too much self-reliance to put up with any sort of spousal betrayal, even from a man she had loved as much as Stephen. Not that she had ever had to deal with such unfaithfulness, or would have had if he were still alive; he had been a fiercely loyal and honorable man, his love for her as steadfast as hers for him.

She redirected the conversation by asking, "Do you know where Dongmei resides?"

"Somewhere in Chinatown, that's all."

"Or anything else about her?"

"No. I didn't want to know anything about her. I still don't."

"You told us yesterday that your husband never confided in you about his connection with the Hip Sing tong. Is that completely true? You have no knowledge at all?"

"None. I swear it."

"Did he ever mention Fowler Alley to you?"

"Fowler Alley? No. Why do you ask that?"

"He spoke the words last night before he was shot."

"That's not significant, is it? It may be where one of his opium dens is located."

"Perhaps," Sabina said. "He spoke two other words as well. 'Blue shadow.' Does that phrase mean anything to you?"

"No, nothing."

"He never used it in your hearing?"

"Never."

"His offices were searched sometime last evening. By you?"

"Of course not. What reason would I have?"

"Where were you before your return home at eight-thirty?"

"At the apothecary shop round the corner. I . . . needed something to help me sleep."

"One more question. Did your husband keep files or other private papers, anything that might pertain to his Hip Sing activities, someplace other than his office?"

"If he did, it wasn't in our home. He was closemouthed, as I told you . . . about everything, including his addiction and his Chinese whore." Andrea Scarlett shifted position, shivering as if with a sudden chill. "That's what makes the attempt on my life so . . . so senseless. I'm no threat to anyone in Chinatown . . . anyone anywhere. What am I going to do, Mrs. Carpenter? I can't go home, I'm afraid to go out in public. . . ."

"You're safe here for the time being, until I can make arrangements for an even more secure refuge."

"When will that be?"

"Soon. Long before nightfall. You'll be well protected."

"Well protected." Bitterness had crept back into the woman's voice. "Your partner wasn't able to protect James last night, was he?"

"That's uncalled for, Mrs. Scarlett. He had to carry your husband out of the resort and was taking him to your home when the highbinder struck. Burdened as he was, he had no time to prevent what happened. He was almost killed himself."

There were several seconds of silence. Then, "Yes, you're right, I'm sorry. It's just that I'm so frightened. I don't want to die as James did, and for something I had nothing to do with and know nothing about. . . ."

Hunger gnawed at Sabina when she left the rooming house. Except for the months following Stephen's death, she had always had a prodigious appetite and all she'd had to eat today were an egg and two slices of bread with marmalade for breakfast. She'd have liked to stop into a café or teashop for a quick bite, but she would have to wait to fill the hollow in her stomach. Wait, too, to contact Elizabeth Petrie, a former police matron who could be counted on to keep a sharp protective eye on their client; Andrea Scarlett would be safe enough where she was for another few daylight hours. As it was, Sabina had just enough time to get to the Blanchford estate on Nob Hill and punctually keep her one-thirty appointment with the financier's widow.

6
SABINA

"No, no, no." Harriet Blanchford leaned forward to tap Sabina smartly on the knee with a bony forefinger. "Infernal devices, telephones. Bad connections are the norm, so everything gets mixed up. I did not say I wished to hire your agency because my husband has been kidnapped. I said I wished to hire you because my husband's *body* has been kidnapped."

"His . . . body?"

"From the family mausoleum, though neither Bertram nor I can imagine how it was done. Quite impossible, and yet there you are. They're demanding seventy-five thousand dollars."

"Who is?"

An impatient frown creased Mrs. Blanchford's crepelike countenance. "The scoundrels responsible, of course," she said. "Perhaps it wasn't the telephone after all. Are you hard of hearing, young woman?"

"Not to my knowledge."

"Then kindly pay attention."

Harriet Blanchford was a somewhat frail woman in her seventies, pallid and hollow-eyed, dressed entirely in mourning black, but obviously strong-willed, determined, and in full possession of her faculties. It was also obvious that she ruled this grand Nob Hill home, now inhabited by her and her son Bertram, and no doubt had even when her husband was alive.

Sabina said, "Yes, ma'am," and resisted an urge to remove her jacket, loosen the tight collar of her shirtwaist, or both. The manse's drawing room was as warm as the oven room of a bakery, with all the windows closed and a fire blazing on the hearth even though the weather today was on the balmy side. It also smelled unpleasantly of potpourri mingled with woodsmoke and fumes from the oversweet violet sachet Mrs. Blanchford favored.

Another case of body snatching, this time for ransom.

A bizarre coincidence, surely; it seemed inconceivable that there could be a connection between the abduction of the Chinese tong leader's remains and the disappearance of the shell of the late Ruben Blanchford. But no matter what was behind it,

Sabina found the grieving widow's plight to be both intriguing and challenging. So would John when she told him.

"A heinous crime, indeed," she said. "The more so for having taken place so soon after your bereavement. You must be devastated."

"We are. Or at least I am," Mrs. Blanchford added, glancing at her son.

"Now, Mother." Bertram Blanchford, who was seated on another of the room's ornate and uncomfortable chairs, was a plump, balding, clean-shaven man in his forties, dressed in an expensive broadcloth suit as mourning-black as his mother's velveteen dress. "Father and I may not have gotten along, but you know I'm as upset as you are."

"About the kidnapping, yes, but not that he's gone to his reward. He lingered at death's door for weeks before passing through and you gave him little enough comfort."

"How could I? You're the only one he wanted at his bedside."

Sabina cleared her throat. "About the, ah, kidnapping," she said to Mrs. Blanchford. "Have you any idea who is responsible?"

"Ghouls, that's who. Monsters preying on the bereaved and grief-stricken."

"Yes. But I meant anyone in particular, by name."

"No one we know could conceivably be involved," Bertram said. "Blackguards from the Barbary Coast is my guess, drawn by the funeral notices in the newspapers. The kind that will stop at nothing, including violence against those who deny them."

His mother sniffed. "You keep saying that, Bertram. It sounds as though you're well acquainted with the Devil's Playground."

"Hardly. But you and I both know its evil reputation."

"The racetrack touts and bookmakers you consort with are no better."

"Now, Mother, you know that's not true . . ."

"Do I?" She thumped the edge of her hand on a stack of magazines on a table between their chairs. "What do you call this trash you insist on bringing into the house?"

"The *Breeder and Sportsman* is a respectable publication, devoted to people of culture and refinement who admire the sport of kings —"

"Balderdash. Sport of kings! Greedy humans exciting themselves by betting on sweaty animals chasing each other around an oval of dirt and mud." Then, to Sabina,

"My son thinks we ought to pay the ransom."

"Yes, I do," Bertram said. "It's the only way to ensure a safe return."

"Do you agree, Mrs. Carpenter?"

"I'm afraid not. Paying a ransom demand is a poor risk in any case."

"That is my position as well, at least for the present. I'll have no rest until my husband's remains are back where they belong, and none, either, until the perpetrators of this outrage are exposed and punished. That is why you're here. I have been told you and your partner are competent detectives. The most competent in the city, would you say?"

John would, in a heartbeat. Sabina was, as always, more discreet. "We have had considerable success in our investigations. If you would like references, I can give you the names of several satisfied clients —"

"No, no, that isn't necessary. I'm already aware of your credentials, though I must say I don't understand why an attractive young widow would wish to undertake such a profession."

"My late husband and I were both employed by the Pinkerton Detective Agency when we met. I was not their first women operative, nor the last. More women every year are entering into one facet of law enforcement or another, and proving just as capable as their male counterparts."

"Mmm, yes. Well, I'm not sure I approve, but I admit to being old-fashioned when it comes to our sex. What assurances can you give me that you'll succeed in finding my husband and punishing his abductors?"

"None except that we will make every possible effort to do so."

"A proper answer. Yes, you'll do."

"Thank you." Sabina shifted on the hard cushion of her chair, seeking — and not finding — some relief from the heat of the fire. "Do you have any idea when the theft took place?"

"One of the last two nights," Bertram said. "Father was laid to rest in the mausoleum on Monday."

"Have you informed the police?"

"Certainly not," Mrs. Blanchford said. "Ruben considered the police inept and corrupt, and I quite agree." So did John, despite his recent dealings with them, and Sabina concurred, though to a lesser extent. "And their involvement would bring the worst sort of sensational publicity, the likes of which I wish to avoid at all cost."

"Quite understandable. When did you receive the ransom note?"

"This morning. It was in a package Edmund found on the doorstep."

"Edmund?"

"My houseman. That package, there on the table."

Sabina had noticed it before, lying atop the equestrian publications, and now she looked at it more closely. It consisted of a small cardboard box with a closed lid, resting in a nest of torn brown wrapping paper and string.

"Go ahead, young woman. Open it."

The box contained a large sheet of folded paper, a raggedly cut triangle of white satin, and a large gold ring with a distinctive ruby setting. Sabina unfolded the paper. Crude, childlike writing covered it on a downward slant. The message was brief and to the point.

We have your husbans body. Hidden where nobuddy can find it. $75,000 in large greenbaks or youll never see agin. Instrukshuns soon. No coppers or else!

Disguised writing? Faked illiteracy? Possibly, but Sabina couldn't be certain in either case.

She asked Mrs. Blanchford, "The ring belonged to your late husband, I take it?"

"Certainly. I gave it to him as an anniversary present many years ago. It was interred with him."

"And the piece of satin — cut from the lining of his casket?"

"Yes."

Bertram added, "As soon as we opened the package and read the note, Mother and Edmund and I went straightaway to the mausoleum. We found the door locked and apparently undisturbed. If it hadn't been for the ring and the piece of casket cloth, we would have considered the whole business a monstrous hoax."

"What did you do then?"

"Bertram and I went downtown to Whitburn Trust to get the mausoleum key," Mrs. Blanchford said. "After the funeral I put it in my box in the bank for safekeeping."

"Is that the only key?"

"Yes, the only one."

"And no one has access to the safe box but you and your son?"

"No one but me. The box was my husband's and mine. Its contents are of no concern to anyone else, even my son, as long as I am alive."

Bertram made a sound that might have been a stifled sigh. "You can imagine how we felt when we returned and entered the mausoleum and found the casket empty."

"And this piece of satin fit into the hole cut in the lining?"

"An exact fit."

"Devil's work," Mrs. Blanchford said. "Almost as if entry had been gained and Ruben spirited away by supernatural means."

"Mother believes in spiritualism," Bertram said to Sabina.

"Spiritualism, yes. Demonic ghouls, no. I said 'as if,' didn't I? No, by heaven, whoever committed this atrocity is human and damnably clever."

"And potentially dangerous to your safety and mine."

The long-suffering look Harriet Blanchford aimed in Sabina's direction told her she wasn't the only one who considered Bertram a weakling and likely a coward. The opposite of his strong, feisty mother — an admirable woman despite her old-fashioned attitudes.

"I'll have a look at the mausoleum now, Mrs. Blanchford, if your son will show me the way."

The old woman produced a large key from the pocket of her dress, placed it in Sabina's, not her son's, hand. Bertram's lips tightened; he rose stiffly from his chair. He, too, was aware of what she thought of him.

He left the parlor to fetch a lantern, and when he returned he led the way through French doors onto a terrace surrounded by an opulent garden dominated by rosebushes and yew trees. The cool air was a relief after the overheated parlor. Although she was practical to a fault while engaged in a business matter, Sabina couldn't help but admire the sweeping views. The Marin headlands, the bay and the military garrison on Alcatraz Island, the forest of masts on the sailing ships crowding the piers and warehouses along the Embarcadero — all were visible in the bright afternoon sunlight.

Nor could she help wondering, briefly, what it would be like to live in such lofty surroundings as these. One day, perhaps, if Carpenter and Quincannon, Professional Detective Services, continued to flourish and she were ever to remarry, she would find out. That thought brought a familiar handsome face to mind, and she quickly shuttered it. Curiously, and a little discomfitingly, the image had been John's, not Carson Montgomery's.

The mausoleum stood at the opposite end of the garden, at the bottom of a short incline — a square, squat, moss-coated stone structure with no external markings.

Nearby stood a carriage barn, behind which a carriageway led to a cross street beyond. The Blanchfords' nearest neighbor in that direction, Sabina noted, looked to be several hundred yards distant. Simple enough, then, for the body snatchers to have driven a wagon in and parked it directly behind the crypt. Done in the dead of night, they would have little fear of being seen.

The door set into the mausoleum's facing wall was made of filigreed bronze and appeared to be several inches thick. Sabina had learned about locks while a Pink Rose, from Stephen and later from experience; she bent immediately to examine the one here, peering at it through the small magnifying glass she carried in her bag. There were no indications that lock picks or any other tool had been used on it. The only marks were light nicks made by the key when it was inserted into the lock. Nor had the hinges been tampered with in any way.

Could a skeleton key have been used? No, not on a lock of this age and type, unless the original locksmith was involved in the abduction. A possibility to be checked, but a highly unlikely one.

"This door is the only way in or out?" she asked Bertram.

"Yes. No windows, of course, or any aper-
tures."

"I'll have a look just the same."

"Are you sure you want to go inside, Mrs.
Carpenter? There's really nothing to see,
and it's rather dank and unclean."

"Yes, I'm sure. I've been in much less
desirable places."

"But your clothing . . ."

She pressed the key into his hand. "Open
the door, please."

Bertram shrugged and fired the lantern's
wick before sliding the heavy key into the
lock and turning the bolt. The door was as
heavy as it looked; it took a bit of effort to
swing it open. The hinges creaked, but not
loudly enough for the sound to carry even
at night. The walls were thick and well
sealed, the atmosphere as dank and cob-
webby as Bertram had indicated.

He handed the lantern to her, saying, "I'll
wait here, if you don't mind."

She stepped into the gloomy interior,
holding the lantern aloft. By its flickering
light she could see four stone biers arranged
along the walls. Bronze coffins rested on
two of them, both with their lids closed.
One of them was small; she went to that
one first. Engraved on a silver plate on its
side was the name Jennifer Blanchford and

the dates 1872–1886.

"My younger sister Jenny," Bertram said from the doorway. "She died of consumption."

"Her casket wasn't disturbed?"

"No. The lid is still tightly bolted, as you can see."

Sabina went to examine the second coffin. It was one of the largest and most elaborate she had ever seen, with knobs, hinges, and handles made of pure silver. The silver plate on its side bore Ruben Blanchford's name and the dates of his birth and death. She grasped the handle, and found the lid heavier than expected when she tried to raise it.

Bertram came to her assistance. The lid had been screwed down and the screws removed without damage, she noted. There was a hole in its satin lining where the triangular piece had been neatly cut out. The satin ruffles covering the sides were unmarked. She ran fingertips over the satin-pillowed bed, which was smooth and un-wrinkled.

While he lowered the lid again, she bent with the lantern to study the stone floor around the bier. Nothing there caught her eye — no marks, no objects of any kind. An examination of the walls confirmed that they were all solid, inches thick like the door, with not so much as a tiny chink in the mortar between the stones.

Outside again, as Bertram swung the heavy door shut and relocked it, Sabina asked him, "Was the lid on your father's casket open or closed when you and Edmund first entered the crypt?"

"What possible difference can that make?"

"Open or closed, sir?"

"Closed." Bertram frowned. "Have you an idea of how the deed was done?"

"I've only just begun my investigation, Mr. Blanchford. Any ideas I might have at this point are premature."

She took the key from him, without any fuss on his part, as they started back to the house. Mrs. Blanchford had entrusted it to her and she would be the one to return it. Her credo had always been and always would be to never violate even the smallest trust.

7
QUINCANNON

Upon leaving the agency Quincannon rode a streetcar up Market to Van Ness Avenue, from where he walked the short distance to Hayes Street and St. Ignatius College. The Jesuit school had grown considerably since being granted a state charter in 1859 and had moved to this location some fifteen years earlier. It had several hundred students and a faculty that included Father James O'Halloran, whom Quincannon had had the pleasure of meeting during an investigation two years before.

Father O'Halloran, in addition to other talents, was a student of languages. Quincannon was unsure whether Chinese was among them, but if not, the priest would know someone who could translate the two-page document he'd found in the Mock Don Yuen file in Scarlett's office.

Such was the case. Father O'Halloran's command of the Chinese language was limited, but he knew a scholar fluent in Cantonese and other dialects who should have no difficulty translating the calligraphy. Could this be done as quickly as possible? The priest thought it could. Quincannon left the document with him, with a request that it and the translation be sent to him at the agency by messenger. Although the priest asked for no recompense, Quincannon insisted he accept a five-dollar gold piece — if not for the translation and messenger service, then for the church. Thrifty he might be, but there was also a streak of generosity in his nature that overwhelmed him every now and then.

Next stop: Chinatown.

The Quarter was twelve square blocks of wooden and brick buildings surrounding Portsmouth Square — home to some twenty-five thousand people packed into apartments and rooming houses, business establishments, temples, family associations, bagnios, opium dens, gambling halls. By day it was teeming and noisy, the incense-laden air filled with the clatter of carts and other conveyances on the narrow streets and alleys, the cries of street hawkers, the constant ebb and flow of Cantonese dialects.

Quincannon was one of the few Caucasians in the jostling throng as he made his way along Dupont Avenue, Chinatown's main thoroughfare, named after a naval admiral when California was admitted to the Union in 1846. The Chinese called it "Du Pon Gai." His destination: the herbalist shop owned by Mock Don Yuen.

He would not have been surprised to find the shop closed. Considering the bubbling stew created by the events of the past few days, the venerable new Hip Sing president might well have taken protective refuge in the company's headquarters on Waverly Place. But the shop was open for business — an indication, perhaps, if the tong leader was presiding within, that tensions in the Quarter might not be running quite as high as everyone feared.

Quincannon paused for a few moments before entering. The shop was one of several in a row along one side of a narrow cul-de-sac just off Dupont, most of which had Chinese calligraphy on opaque windows that hid both wares and purpose from Caucasian eyes. Mock Don Yuen's, however, was an exception. English words as well as Chinese characters were written on its window — MOCK DON YUEN, HERBALIST — and the glass itself was transparent enough to reveal a dozen or so varieties of exotic herbs. Each of the plates had a piece of red paper affixed to it, identifying in both languages what it contained: Old Mountain ginseng, ambergris, fossilized lizard teeth, lapis, clove bark, powdered ivory, magpie dung.

There were two doors set side by side in an alcove next to the window. One had a dusty glass pane and opened into the herb shop; the other, hanging slightly crooked in its frame, was solid except for a peephole at eye level. That one, Quincannon thought, would lead upstairs to the room where Mock Don Yuen reputedly ran a gambling parlor in which fantan, mah-jongg, and other games of chance were played for high stakes and the house took a hefty percentage. At the second-story level were three windows with louvered green shutters. No doubt there would be heavy curtains on the inside as an added precaution, and mayhap a spotter stationed somewhere outside in the alley while the richer games were in progress to warn against a possible police raid.

Quincannon opened the shop door and stepped inside to the accompaniment of a small tinkling bell. The interior was not much larger than the parlor of his Leavenworth Street flat, clean and tidy, dimly lighted by a trio of lanterns. On the left was a counter, and behind that, across the entire wall, were blue-lacquered cabinets with hundreds of little drawers. At the rear, heavy bead curtains covered the entrance to an inner room. The front part of the shop was unoccupied when he entered, but a couple of seconds after he shut the door, the bead curtains parted and an aged Chinese appeared, his hands crossed in the voluminous sleeves of a Mandarin robe.

His years numbered at least seventy-five, possibly more, his skin as finely wrinkled as old parchment. His queue was long and pewter-colored, as were the sparse and wispy strands of hair that hung down from each side of his mouth and from his chin like moss on an ancient tree. Rimless, thick-lensed glasses made his rheumy eyes seem overlarge.

He bowed and said in accented but cultured English, "Welcome, most honorable sir. How may I be of service?"

"Are you Mock Don Yuen?"

A nod and another bow.

"John Quincannon. Of Carpenter and Quincannon, Professional Detective Services."

Mock Don Yuen knew the name well enough, but chose not to acknowledge it.

He cocked his head to one side, birdlike, and said in the same polite voice, "Have you an ailment, sir?"

"Ailment?"

"My herbs and tonics are all genuine, imported from the provinces of China. Guaranteed effective for any ailment. You are familiar with Emperor Shen Nung?"

"No."

"He was the ancient father of plants. A thousand years past, in old China, Shen Nung examined many plants to learn their medicinal value. His wisdom, like that of Confucius, has survived the centuries."

"I expect you know why I'm here," Quincannon said, "and it's not to buy herbs and tonics."

"Ah, but they are all that I dispense."

"Information is what I'm after. Like the police, I am investigating the assassination of the Hip Sing attorney James Scarlett last night. On behalf of my client, and as a near victim of the *boo how doy* hatchet man myself."

Mock Don Yuen might have been wearing a mask for all the reaction the name produced. After a few moments he turned away from Quincannon, and without hurry went around behind the counter. He removed one clawlike hand from the sleeve of his robe and ran fingers, the nails of which were some two inches long, over a section of the blue-lacquered cabinet. They came to rest on a drawer a third of the way down. The fragrance of herbs, already strong in the shop, seemed to become even stronger when he opened the drawer.

"May I recommend some lizard tea?" he said. "Most nourishing, a boon to the digestion."

"The police believe that Bin Ah Kee's remains were stolen and Scarlett murdered by Kwong Dock highbinders to provoke a tong war with the Hip Sing. Is that your belief as well?"

Mock Don Yuen opened another drawer. "Gum of the *Koh-liu* from Sumatra? An excellent general tonic."

"Who else might be responsible? Fong Ching?"

Another drawer. "Powdered lily? It has many fine properties. Among them the dispelling of grief, easement of the pain of piles, and the promotion of a male offspring."

Irritably Quincannon said, "I'm not grieving, I don't suffer from piles, and I have no interest in producing an offspring of either sex. Pay mind to me, Mock Don Yuen. No matter who is behind the fomenting of a

107

tong war, you're in a position to prevent it as the Hip Sing's new president."

"Ginseng, sir? Very fine. Ginseng soup, properly brewed, provides strength and a long life."

"No one in Chinatown will have a long life if there's a tong war. I'll warrant you don't want bloodshed any more than I or the police do. I intend to find the men responsible and see them punished. Co-operate with me, and you and the Hip Sing will both benefit."

"Deer's tail from Hwei Chung? Like ginseng, it is one of mankind's greatest blessings."

Blast the man! Quincannon tried a different approach, managing not to scowl or growl as he said, "I know Scarlett was acting as your private counsel. A troublesome legal matter, Mock Don Yuen?"

"Mint leaves? Excellent for combating fire in the human body. Lavender water mixed with ink, for the banishment of headache?"

"Or was it related to the Hip Sing? An expansion of illegal activities, such as the Kwong Dock engages in? Something to do with the disappearance of Bin Ah Kee's remains?"

"Cinnabar, perhaps, for the increase of one's lifespan?"

"Bah!" Quincannon could contain himself no longer. "For all I know *you* arranged the body snatching and Scarlett's assassination — that *you're* the one who wants tong warfare!"

Not even that caused a flicker in the venerable tong leader's impassive calm. "No herbs, sir? No fine tonics? There are more than one thousand prescriptions in the book of Li Shih-chen, the great physician of the Ming dynasty. Those I have mentioned and many others would be of benefit, to assure you health and longevity."

"Better take them yourself, then. You'll need them more than I will."

Behind his thick glasses, Mock Don Yuen's eyes were steady on Quincannon's face. Bird's eyes: it seemed they hadn't blinked once the entire time he'd been there and they didn't blink now.

"You are familiar with Chinese folklore, sir?" he said. "Most interesting. We have sayings appropriate to all occasions. For instance there is that which states, 'Loud bark, no good dogs; loud talk, no wise man.' "

Quincannon forbore offering up one of several pithy and borderline obscene Western sayings that crossed his mind, turned on his heel, and left the shop. The tinkling of the bell over the door as he went out was not unlike the sound of mocking laughter.

8
QUINCANNON

Fowler Alley was a typical Chinatown passage: narrow, crooked, packed with long-pigtailed men and women mostly dressed in the black clothing of the lower-caste Chinese. Brightly hued paper lanterns strung along rickety balconies and the glowing braziers of food sellers added the only color and light to a tunnellike expanse made even gloomier by the day's overcast sky.

Quincannon wandered along, gazing at storefronts and the upper floors of sagging firetraps roofed in tarpaper and gravel. Many of the second and third floors were private apartments, hidden from view behind dusty, curtained windows. Some of the business establishments were identifiable from their displayed wares: restaurants flying three-cornered yellow silk pennants, herb shops, a clothiers, a vegetable market. Others, tucked away behind closed doors, darkened windows, and signs in Chinese characters remained a mystery.

Nothing in the alley aroused his suspicions or pricked his curiosity. There were no tong headquarters here, as Price had made clear last night; no opium resorts or sporting houses; and nothing even remotely suggestive of blue shadows. One of the Hip Sing's fantan parlors might be operating here, but even if so, there would seem to be little connection between the tong's gambling enterprise and James Scarlett's last words.

Quincannon retraced his steps through the passage, stopping the one other white man he saw and several Chinese. Did anyone know Scarlett, the Hip Sing attorney? The Caucasian was a dry-goods drummer on his second and what he obviously hoped would be his last visit to the Quarter; he had never heard of Scarlett, he said. All the Chinese either didn't speak English or pretended they didn't.

Fowler Alley lay open on both ends, debouching into other passages, but at least for the present, Quincannon thought bleakly as he left it, it was a dead end.

Once called Pike Street, Waverly Place was one of Chinatown's more notorious thoroughfares. Here, temples and fraternal buildings stood cheek by jowl with opium and gambling dens and the cribs of the flower willows. Last night, when Quincannon had started his hunt for James Scarlett, the passage had been mostly empty; by daylight it teemed with carts, wagons, buggies, half-starved dogs and cats, and human pedestrians. The noise level was as high and constant as that on Dupont Avenue, a shrill tide dominated by the lilting dialects of Canton, Shanghai, and the provinces of Old China.

Two doors down from the three-story tong building was the Four Families Temple, a building of equal height but with a much more ornate façade, its balconies carved and painted and decorated with pagoda cornices. On impulse Quincannon turned in through the entrance doors and proceeded along a narrow passage to what was known as the Hall of Sorrows, where funeral services were conducted and the bodies of the deceased highborn were laid out in their caskets for viewing.

Candlelight flickered; the pungent odor of incense assailed his nostrils. The long room, deserted at the moment, was ceiled with a massive scrolled wood carving covered in gold leaf, from which hung dozens of lanterns in pink and green, red and gold. At the far end were a pair of large altars, a red prayer bench fronting one. Smaller altars on either side wore embroidered cloths on which fruit, flowers, candles, and joss urns had been arranged.

It must have been in the vicinity of those altars that the remains of Bing Ah Kee had lain. The thieves had slithered in sometime during the early morning hours and pried up the lid of his coffin, sealed after the last viewing, in order to make off with the corpse — a risky venture even in the middle of the night. At least four men had to have been involved, two to remove the body, a third to act as lookout, and a fourth to drive whatever conveyance was used. Such a mission required careful planning, and careful planning meant a definite purpose. Yet no word of the body snatchers' intentions had been forthcoming — none, that was, that had as yet reached Occidental ears.

The ground floor of the Hip Sing Company was a fraternal gathering place, open to the street; the two upper floors, where tong business was conducted, were closed off to visitors and would be well guarded. Quincannon entered freely, passed down a corridor into a large common room. Several black-garbed men, most of them elderly, were playing mah-jongg at a table at one end. Other men sat on cushions and benches, sipping tea, smoking, reading Chinese-language newspapers. A few cast wary glances at the Occidental intruder, but most ignored him.

A middle-aged fellow, his skull completely bald except for a long, braided queue that extended below his shoulder blades, approached him, bowed, and asked in halting English, "There is something the gentleman seeks?"

Quincannon said, "An audience with Mock Quan," and handed over one of his business cards.

"Please to wait here, honorable sir." The Chinese bowed again, took the card away through a doorway covered by a worn silk tapestry.

Quincannon waited. No one paid him the slightest attention now. He was loading his pipe when the bald man returned and said, "You will follow me, please."

They passed through the tapestried doorway, up a stairway so narrow Quincannon had to turn his body slightly as he ascended. Another man waited at the top, this one young, thickset, with a curved scar under one eye and both hands hidden inside the voluminous sleeves of his blouse. Highbinder on guard duty: Those sleeves would conceal revolver or knife or short, sharp hatchet, or possibly all three.

As the bald one retreated down the stairs, the highbinder and "foreign devil" eyed each other impassively. Quincannon had no intention of relinquishing his Navy Colt; if any effort were made to search him, he would draw the weapon and take his chances. But the guard made no such attempt. In swift, gliding movements he turned and went sideways along a hallway, his gaze on Quincannon all the while. At an open doorway at the far end, he paused and stood aside, stiff and straight as if at attention. When Quincannon entered the room beyond, the highbinder filled the doorway behind him as effectively as any panel of wood.

The chamber might have been an office in any building in San Francisco. There was a long, high desk, a safe, several stools, a round table set with a tea service. The only Oriental touches were a red silk wall tapestry embroidered with threads of gold, a statue of Buddha, and an incense bowl that emitted a rich, spicy scent. Lamplight highlighted the face of the man standing behind the desk — a man of no more than thirty, slender, clean-shaven, his hair worn long but unqueued, Western style, his body encased in a robe of red brocaded silk that

116

didn't quite conceal the shirt and string tie underneath.

"I am Mock Quan," he said. His English was unaccented and precise. "It is I with whom you wish to speak, not my honorable father?"

"I've already spoken with Mock Don Yuen at his shop."

"About what, may I ask?"

"The murder of James Scarlett."

"And was it a satisfactory conversation?"

"It would have been if I was interested in buying herbs."

"Ah. So now you have come to me. But I fear you have wasted your time, Mr. Quincannon. I know nothing about the unfortunate incident in Ross Alley."

"Would you tell me if you did?"

"The best interests of the Hip Sing Company are for the council of elders and my father to decide, not I."

"That's not what I asked you."

"A man of my lowly station has few answers to important questions. On this matter I have none."

"Lowly station, Mock Quan? The ambitious son of the Hip Sing's new president?"

A slight lifting of one shoulder. "Ambition in a young man does not mean he is worthy."

Horseapples, Quincannon thought. He smiled, the kind of razor-edged smile that had caused many a man to begin quaking in his boots. Not this young rascal, however.

"No more evasions, Mock Quan. We both know James Scarlett was murdered by a Hip Sing highbinder."

"Your assumptions are false. The Hip Sing would never countenance the assassination of an Occidental."

"No? Then who would?"

"The Kwong Dock and their cowardly leader, Fong Ching." The response came quickly, without hesitation. So much for Mock Quan's man-of-lowly-station-with-no-answers pose.

"Why would they want Scarlett dead?"

"He was acting counsel for the Hip Sing Company and as such privileged to certain confidences. You are surely aware of this."

"I am. I also know that one of his clients was your father. The question is in what capacity."

"That is no concern of yours, Mr. Quincannon."

"It is if it has a bearing on Scarlett's murder."

"It does not. The unfortunate Mr. Scarlett had become a slave to *ah pin vin;* it may be that the drug clouded his judgment, made

118

him unstable enough to betray his trust and sell out to the Kwong Dock. If so, he was an expendable pawn in Fong Ching's vicious and unscrupulous hunger for power." The young Chinese's lips thinned as he spoke. "Fong Ching hates and fears the Hip Sing Company, for we are stronger than any of the tongs under his yoke. He wishes to destroy the Hip Sing so he may reign as king of Chinatown."

"He's the king now, isn't he?"

"No!" Mock Quan's anger came like the sudden flare of a match. Almost as quickly it was extinguished, but not before Quincannon had a glimpse beneath the cultured façade. "He is a fat jackal in lion's skin, the son of a turtle."

That last statement revealed the depth of Mock Quan's loathing for Little Pete; it was the bitterest of Chinese insults. Quincannon said, "Jackals feed on the dead. The dead such as Bing Ah Kee?"

"Oh, yes, it is beyond question Fong Ching is responsible for that outrage."

"What do you suppose was done with the body?"

Mock Quan made a slicing gesture with one slim hand. "Should the vessel of the honorable Bing Ah Kee have been harmed in any fashion, may Fong Ching suffer the death of a thousand cuts ten thousand times through eternity."

"If the Hip Sing is so sure he's responsible, why has nothing been done to retaliate?"

"Without proof of Fong Ching's treachery, the decision of the council of elders was that the wisest course was to withhold a declaration of war."

"Even after what happened to James Scarlett? His murder could be termed an act of open aggression."

"Mr. Scarlett was neither Chinese nor a member of the Hip Sing Company, merely an employee. Evidently an untrustworthy one." Mock Quan took a tailor-made cigarette from a box on his desk, fitted it into a carved ivory holder. "The council of elders met again this morning. It was decided then to permit the American Terror, Lieutenant Price, and his raiders to punish Fong Ching and the Kwong Dock, thus to avoid the shedding of Hip Sing blood. This will soon be done."

"What makes you so certain?"

"It is the only way to crush the life from the turtle's offspring and prevent tong bloodshed."

"Did you have a say in the council's decision?"

The question discomfited Mock Quan.

His eyes narrowed; he exhaled smoke in a thin jet. "I am not privileged to sit on the council of elders."

"But I'll wager you have your father's confidence as well as his ear, and that your powers of persuasion are considerable."

"Such matters do not concern you."

"Anything relating to Scarlett's murder concerns me," Quincannon said. "I was nearly shot, too, in Ross Alley. And I'm not as convinced as you are that Little Pete is behind the death of James Scarlett or the disappearance of Bing Ah Kee's remains."

Mock Quan made an odd hissing sound with his lips, a Chinese expression of anger and contempt. There was less oil and more steel in his voice when he spoke again. "You would do well to bow to the superior workings of the police, lest your blood stain a Chinatown alley after all."

"I don't like warnings, Mock Quan, much less threats."

"A lowly Chinese warn or threaten a distinguished Occidental detective? My words were merely ones of caution and prudence."

Quincannon's smile this time was a thin lip-stretch. He said, "I have no intention of leaving a single drop of my blood in Chinatown or anywhere else in this city."

"Then you would be wise not to venture here again after the cloak of night has fallen." Mock Quan smiled in return, his as counterfeit as Quincannon's. So was the invitation which followed. "Will you join me in a cup of excellent rose-petal tea before you leave?"

"Another time, perhaps."

"Perhaps. *Ho hang la* — I hope you have a safe walk."

Quincannon said, lying in his teeth, "Health and a long life to you, too, Mock Quan."

On his way out of Chinatown, a shouting newsboy drew his attention to the fact that the *Evening Bulletin* had appeared. He bought a copy and glanced over the front page. Hell, damn, and blast! As he'd feared, some copper at the Hall of Justice had leaked his name to that scoundrel Homer Keeps. The bold headlines caused his blood pressure to soar.

One of them read: NOTORIOUS PRIVATE DETECTIVE IMPLICATED IN CHINATOWN SLAYING. Notorious! The story, which of course bore Keeps's byline, was even more outrageous — littered with allusions to Quincannon's "history of blatant disregard for human life," "past excursions into the city's netherworld of violence," and "escapades of dubious legitimacy," and with sly insinuations that he was partly to blame for James Scarlett's death and that his presence at the opium resort indicated he, too, might be a "dude fiend" hop smoker. Altogether it amounted to another of Keeps's deliberate attempts at character assassination — potentially damaging not only to Quincannon's personal reputation but to that of Carpenter and Quincannon, Professional Detective Services. And yet so carefully worded that it was not quite actionable.

Damn Homer bloody Keeps! If the little bastard had been nearby just then, he might well have ended up strangled, shot, or severely maimed.

9
SABINA

Sabina's first stop after leaving the Blanchford estate was the Hyde Street home of Elizabeth Petrie. As was usually the case, the former police matron was in residence, working on one of her finely crafted quilts. Quilting had been her profession for several years, ever since her police inspector husband, Oliver, was implicated in a corruption scandal that resulted in a one-year prison sentence. Although Elizabeth had had no knowledge of his grafting activities, the scandal's taint had cost her her matron's job. And brought an end to what had been a stormy marriage marred by Oliver's fondness for strong drink. He had drowned himself in whiskey after his release from Folsom, and eventually died of acute alcoholism. Ironically, the house Elizabeth had shared with him and where she still resided was only a short distance from the Home for Inebriates at Chestnut and Stockton

Streets, where many of the city's once respectable citizens drew their final breaths.

Police work was in Elizabeth's blood, and she had made it known to the private investigative agencies in the city that whenever a woman operative was needed, she would be available. In her middle forties, with graying hair perpetually worn in a bun, she had a grandmotherly air that concealed a sharp-witted, no-nonsense interior. Sabina had availed of her services on three previous occasions, and found her to be competent, fearless, and completely trustworthy.

Once the situation with Andrea Scarlett was explained to her, Elizabeth eagerly agreed to act as the woman's protector for as long as necessary. She would leave immediately for Delilah Brown's Pine Street rooming house, taking a loaded pistol with her, and bring Mrs. Scarlett back here to her home for safekeeping. The fact that she was a quilter and the client a former seamstress provided a common ground that should also help to ease Mrs. Scarlett's fright.

From Hyde, Sabina proceeded downtown to the newsstand presided over by a "blind" vendor known as Slewfoot, who, in addition to dispensing newspapers and magazines, gathered information on various illegal and extralegal activities throughout the city and served as one of her and John's most reliable informants. Armed with two recent back issues of the *Morning Call,* she then returned to the agency offices.

John was not there, nor had he been, evidently, since this morning. Still trekking about in Chinatown, no doubt — without his customary recklessness, she hoped. As much as she chided him for his interest in her personal life, she couldn't help feeling a concern for his well-being that went beyond their business arrangement. Sometimes, she admitted to herself, it approached fondness. If only he weren't such a determined lecher. Well, perhaps "lecher" was too strong a word. Seduction was not all that was on his mind in his constant efforts to woo her affection; she knew his feelings for her went deeper than that. Which was the primary reason she took such pains to hold him at bay. Business and pleasure simply did not mix, particularly with two strong-willed and differently oriented individuals.

She concentrated on the back issues of the *Call.* The first, four days old, carried the announcement of Ruben Blanchford's death by heart failure after a lengthy illness, at the age of sixty-four. The obituary was accompanied by a photograph that matched

126

Sabina's memory of the man at their single meeting: slight of build with iron-gray hair thinning on top, gray muttonchop whiskers, and large ears set at an angle to his head. He had been quite short, too, she recalled, less than five and a half feet tall. The only information the obit supplied that she didn't already know was the family's estimated net worth — ten million, a figure that would put an avaricious gleam in John's eye when he learned of it — and Bertram Blanchford's profession, obliquely stated as "promoter." He was also described as being "well-known among the sporting set."

The issue dated two days later carried a story about the Blanchford funeral, which seemed to have been less elaborately staged than the reporter expected. The account provided the identity of the mortuary where it had taken place — Joshua Trilby's Evergreen Chapel, with an address on Mission Street — and the names of the prominent citizens who had attended and those who had acted as pallbearers. Three of the pallbearers were familiar, all wealthy businessmen in Ruben Blanchford's class. One of the unfamiliar names, Thomas Moody, was listed as managing director of the Blanchford Investment Foundation.

The foundation's address was given as

512 Pine Street, which would put it in the heart of the financial district — only a few blocks' walk from the agency offices. Sabina examined herself in her compact mirror, re-pinned a few stray wisps of hair that had come loose, added a touch of rouge to her cheeks, and decided she looked presentable enough. A brief message for John, in the event he returned before she did, and she was on her way to the center of San Francisco's commerce.

The offices of the Blanchford Investment Foundation were on the ground floor of a two-story brick building ornamented with curvilinear pediments over its windows and cornices supported on decorative brackets. Little enough money had been spent on BIF's décor or furnishings; the anteroom was small and functional, as was the middle-aged woman who presided over it. One of Sabina's business cards and a message that she was in the employ of Mrs. Harriet Blanchford brought her an immediate audience with Thomas Moody in the managing director's equally Spartan private office.

"I can't imagine why Mrs. Blanchford would need the service of a private investigator," Moody said. His eyes and the prim set of his mouth added the phrase "And a woman, at that." He was a spare, clean-shaven man in his fifties with thin, pinched features and a priggish air.

"A private matter," Sabina told him. "If you'd care to telephone Mrs. Blanchford to confirm her engagement of my services . . ."

"No, no, that won't be necessary. How may I help you?"

"I understand you were one of the pall-bearers at Mr. Blanchford's funeral."

If Moody found the question odd, he didn't show it. His thin face assumed a dolorous expression. "I had that sad honor, yes. He was a friend of long standing as well as my employer."

"I understand it was quite well attended."

"The funeral? Oh, yes. Mr. Blanchford had many friends and associates in the city."

"I'm not familiar with Joshua Trilby's Evergreen Chapel. I assume it's a first-class establishment?"

"Ah, I wouldn't say that, no."

"Really? Why not?"

"Well . . ." Moody lowered his voice, after the fashion of a man about to reveal a confidence. "Rather small and . . . well, somewhat less suitable than one might have hoped for a man of Mr. Blanchford's stature."

"How so?"

"Well, for one thing, Mr. Blanchford didn't look as . . . natural as he might have. Rather a slipshod job, in my opinion. The viewing room was small and the floral offerings haphazardly arranged."

Thus confirming the *Call* reporter's comment. "A shame. Was the procession properly handled?"

"More or less, except for the delay."

"Delay?"

"After the service. Some sort of difficulty with the hearse that kept us all waiting for ten minutes before the casket could be carried out. Poor Mrs. Blanchford . . . she wept the entire time."

"Unconscionable," Sabina said. "Was it she who chose the Trilby mortuary?"

"I suppose it must have been." Moody seemed to feel that perhaps he'd been too candid in his remarks. He made haste to change the subject. "Such a great loss to us all, especially those who have benefited and will continue to benefit from Mr. Blanchford's philanthropic endeavors. He was a fine man, generous and caring to a fault."

"His widow seems to be cut from the same cloth."

"Oh, yes. A wonderful woman."

"And his son?"

Moody hesitated before he said, a trifle

stiffly, "Yes, of course."

"Is Bertram Blanchford involved in the foundation's work?"

"No. No, he isn't."

"By his choice? Or his father's?"

Another hesitation, longer this time. Moody's nose and upper lip quivered in a way that made Sabina think of a disapproving rabbit. "I believe his interests lie elsewhere."

"Bertram is a promoter and horse racing enthusiast, I understand. What does he promote?"

"I'm sure I have no idea."

Sabina thought that this was an evasion, judging from the way Moody's gaze shifted. But she didn't press him. "Well, I don't suppose it matters," she said. "I expect his father left him well provided for, even though they didn't get on well together."

"I really couldn't say, Mrs. Carpenter. I hardly know the man."

A modest sign on the rectangle of lawn in front of Joshua Trilby's Evergreen Chapel gave its name and the slogan HONORING YOUR FAMILY'S MEMORIES. The mortuary itself, a whitewashed wooden structure with a pair of large yew trees flanking the front entrance, was as unprepossessing as Thomas

Moody's description.

On impulse, Sabina followed a cobbled path to the door and stepped into a spacious foyer. A strong floral scent greeted her, but it was more than that that set her nostrils twitching. She had always had a sensitive sense of smell and mingled with the flowery sweetness she detected the odors of dust and, faintly and unpleasantly, formaldehyde. An open doorway to her left led into a viewing room where a rather plain coffin, its lid raised, rested on a bier surrounded by several bouquets of flowers. None of a grouping of chairs facing the coffin was occupied.

Two other doors, both closed, opened off the foyer. Almost immediately one of them opened and a small, pink-faced man appeared. He wore a black cutaway coat and striped trousers and a smile that struck Sabina as both grave and unctuous. As he approached her, he held his hands close together in front of him as if he might start wringing them at any second.

"Ah, good afternoon, madam," he said in a low voice that matched his smile. "How may I be of service?"

"Are you Mr. Trilby? Joshua Trilby?"

"I am. Yes, indeed." He bowed slightly. "Pray tell, is it a recent bereavement that brings you to the Evergreen Chapel?"

The thinly concealed eagerness in Trilby's voice was off-putting. So was his manner. Morticians by trade were a fawning lot, but this one oozed greed as well as obsequiousness.

"Not exactly," she said. "At least . . . not yet."

"Ah. I understand. And you would like to make arrangements in advance of the, ah, unfortunate passage."

"Yes, but I haven't made up my mind as to where the services will be held. Your fees are competitive, I trust?"

"Oh, indeed. Yes, indeed. Quite competitive. We offer a wide array of services designed to accommodate every pocketbook. May I ask what type of ceremony you had in mind, large or small?"

"Large enough. I understand you held the service for the recently deceased financier Ruben Blanchford."

Trilby beamed at her. "Yes, we did. A beautiful service, if I do say so myself. Really quite beautiful."

"And expensive, no doubt."

"Well . . . Mr. Blanchford was an important man in this life. Naturally his passage into the next demanded nothing less than the very best."

"Naturally. Was it his widow who made the arrangements with you?"

"Why, yes, certainly. The casket she chose was our finest model, bronze with silver fittings and duchesse satin interior." Trilby's greed oozed through again. "Is that the sort you had in mind for your loved one, Mrs., ah, Mrs. —"

"Dalrymple," Sabina said. "Lucrezia Dalrymple. How much would such a casket cost?"

"One thousand dollars. Yes, and a bargain at the price, I assure you. We have one in our showroom, if you'd like to see it."

"That won't be necessary."

"Of course we also have other, less elegant models," Trilby said quickly. "Several, in fact, priced to fit any pocketbook."

"I'm sure you do."

"Our entire selection is available for viewing. I also have a complete list of all-inclusive fees for our services which I will gladly —"

"Perhaps another time. I really must be going now."

Trilby's smile flickered. "But Mrs. Dalrymple —"

"Good-bye for now, Mr. Trilby."

She left him actually wringing his hands, a commingled look of bewilderment and dejection on his too-pink face. Nothing upset a man who clearly worshipped the almighty dollar more than having the prospect of a lucrative transaction snatched away from him for no apparent reason.

10
SABINA

It was a quarter of six when Sabina once again returned to the agency offices. This time she found John at his desk, and if not exactly in a cheerful frame of mind, at least glad to see her.

"Ah, my dear, I was hoping you'd return. If you hadn't, I would have called at your rooms this evening."

"Important news, John?"

"No, no. I merely wanted to confer."

"This is the place for business conferences, not my rooms or yours."

"So you've made abundantly clear. You have time now, I trust." His expression altered a bit and his voice was slyly probing when he added, "Unless you have plans for the evening that require you to hurry home?"

Now why would he ask that? Oh, Lord, he hasn't found out I've been keeping company with Carson, has he?

Sabina ignored the question, turning away to shed her coat and hat and then crossing to her desk. She could feel John's eyes on her the entire time. More often than not, one of his unprofessionally covetous gazes nettled her, but today it made her feel uncomfortable in an oddly different way. And a little warm under the high collar of her shirtwaist.

To business, and quickly.

"Did your visit to Fowler Alley prove enlightening?" she asked as she seated herself.

"Not Fowler Alley, no. My call at the Hip Sing Company, yes."

She raised an eyebrow. "You went there? I don't see a puncture wound anywhere. No bullets fired or hatchets or knives thrown your way?"

"Bah. I've bearded fiercer lions in their dens than Mock Quan."

"Mock Quan. Isn't he Mock Don Yuen's son? I thought you intended to see the father."

"I did see him at his herb shop. And learned nothing from him."

"But you did learn something from Mock Quan?"

"Yes. That he's a wily young scoundrel with delusions of grandeur and a hunger for the kind of power Little Pete enjoys."

"Then you think he had something to do with the theft of Bing Ah Kee's remains and the Scarlett murder?"

"Quite possibly, but I can't be sure yet. His father is also suspect, as is Little Pete." John's hands were busy now with the loading and firing of his pipe. When he had it drawing to his satisfaction he asked, "Were you able to track down our client?"

"I was." Sabina explained how she'd found Andrea Scarlett, the reason why the woman had not been at home last night, and her call upon Elizabeth Petrie to act as guardian until the affair was resolved.

The news of the attempt on Mrs. Scarlett's life brought one of John's fierce scowls. "The man who fired the shot at her may or may not have been a Chinese in Western garb? She had no clear impression either way?"

"No. Only a brief glimpse."

"But she is sure the suit he wore was dark-colored?"

"As sure as she could be under the circumstances."

John sat musing for several seconds. Then he blew out a great cloud of tobacco smoke and thumped the desk with his fist. "Dark-colored . . . blue, I wonder? A blue shadow?

Could she have been followed previously by someone wearing clothing of that color?"

"She didn't seem aware of it, if so," Sabina said. "In any event, Scarlett was shot by a highbinder in traditional black Chinese clothing, not one dressed in a blue suit."

"In Chinatown, whereas the attempt on Mrs. Scarlett was made in a white neighborhood. Protective coloration, mayhap."

"That still doesn't explain Scarlett's use of the phrase 'blue shadow.' If in fact that was what he uttered."

"No, it doesn't." Then, after a pause, "Though it might, to an extent, if the assassin was in fact a white man. Scarlett was hardly the only Caucasian on a tong payroll."

"Why would whoever is behind this business use a highbinder for one murder and a white gunman to attempt another?"

"A good question."

"Here's another: How was the highbinder able to follow you on your rounds of the opium resorts?"

"That has been bothering me, too." John shook his head, puffing furiously on his pipe. At length he asked, "Was Mrs. Scarlett able to give you any idea whether her husband kept private papers elsewhere than his office?"

"No."

"Or any other useful information?"

Under different circumstances Sabina might have given him an evasive answer to that question, in order to pursue the matter of Scarlett's Chinese mistress herself. Despite his admonition not to enter Chinatown, there was no real risk in a Caucasian woman walking the Quarter's streets in broad daylight, even in this time of violent unrest. But she would be busy enough as it was with the Blanchford case and her pursuit of information about Carson and the mysterious actions of the bogus Mr. Sherlock Holmes. And the Scarlett case was primarily John's; the fact that he had almost been shot along with the attorney gave him the right to see it through himself.

She said, "Yes, though it may or may not prove significant. It seems her husband had a faithless passion for Chinese women, one named Dongmei in particular."

John's eyes brightened at this. "Well, well. And how did Mrs. Scarlett find out?"

"Apparently he made no secret of the fact. She was hurt, of course, but she cared enough for him, or the income from his Hip Sing activities, to put up with it."

"This Dongmei. A prostitute, one of the flower willows?"

"Possibly a courtesan. Mrs. Scarlett knows little about her, other than the woman was the one who introduced her husband to opium."

"Ah. Before or after he became involved with the Hip Sing?"

"Shortly before, she believes."

"Does she know where Dongmei resides?"

"No."

"I'll find out." John had been scribbling notes to himself. He finished with a flourish, folded the paper, and tucked it into his vest pocket. "Now then — tell me about the rest of your day. You saw the widow Blanchford as scheduled, I trust? And we're now in her employ?"

"Yes to both questions."

"Who was it who was kidnapped?"

"I heard her incorrectly on the telephone," Sabina said. "It was her late husband's body that was abducted. From the family crypt."

"What's that? Another body snatching?"

"Yes."

"For what purpose, in this case?"

"Ransom. Seventy-five thousand dollars for the body's safe return."

She went on to explain about the demand note, the gold ring, and the triangular piece of satin cut from the lining of Ruben Blanchford's coffin. What she didn't confide to him was the seemingly impossible element to the crime. He fancied himself an expert on that sort of mystery, with some past justification, and if he knew about the locked-crypt business he would be sure to insinuate himself into the investigation. This was her case, as the Scarlett homicide was his, and she intended to be the one who solved it.

"Nasty business," he said.

"Nasty and cruel."

His pipe had gone out; he paused to relight it with one of the large sulphur matches he preferred. "First Bing Ah Kee, now Ruben Blanchford. An odd sort of coincidence."

"If it is a coincidence."

"You don't suppose there is any connection? A Chinese tong leader and a wealthy white philanthropist?"

"Not directly, no," Sabina said. "Most likely it was the newspaper reports of the Bing Ah Kee snatch and Ruben Blanchford's death and burial arrangements, both on the same day, that generated the idea."

"Ah. A copycat crime."

"Yes, exactly."

"Have you any leads to the identity of these modern-day William boys?"

"William boys?"

142

"William Burke and William Hare. Irish immigrant murderers hanged in Scotland some seventy years ago. Graverobbers to begin with, supplying doctors at Edinburgh Medical School with dissection cadavers for anatomy lectures. When the supply of newly buried corpses grew short, Burke and Hare turned to murder. Killed sixteen people and sold their remains to a doctor by the name of Knox."

Sabina felt a slight frisson. Mass murder was the most heinous of all crimes, and the impetus for the slaughter John had described struck her as a particularly grisly one.

"Famous case in its day," he went on, "one known to most Scots worldwide. Robert Louis Stevenson wrote a story about the Burkers, as they were called. And children made up a grisly skipping rhyme." Which he proceeded to quote:

Up the close and down the stair,
In the house with Burke and Hare.
Burke's the butcher, Hare's the thief,
Knox, the boy who buys the beef.

"Delightful," Sabina said sardonically. "But to answer your question, no, no direct leads as yet. An idea, however, of where the

143

truth lies and how to go about finding it."

He grinned. "Woman's intuition?"

"Hunch," she said.

Her gaze dared him to argue the semantic distinction. To his credit, he didn't.

"Do you want to discuss it?" he asked.

"No more than you're willing to discuss yours."

11
SABINA

She was even happier than usual to return to her suite of rooms on Russian Hill. It had been a long, tiring day, and she looked forward to settling in for a quiet, contemplative evening and a good night's sleep. Tomorrow promised to be another busy day.

Adam, as always, rushed to meet her. The sharp-eared, long-tailed Abyssinian and Siamese mixture leaped into her arms and briefly cuddled before jumping down and running to his food bowl. Sabina spooned into it some of his favorite fodder, a glutinous, evil-smelling blend her butcher made up for her from God knew what scraps. Satisfied rumbles came from him and his golden fur rippled with pleasure as he tucked into his feast.

She really did need to find him a companion, she thought. He was alone too much. One of the "black, wiggly, and charming" kittens Carson had told her about, perhaps.

In the press of business matters, she'd forgotten about interviewing his relative's litter. She would have to remind him when she saw him again on Saturday night for their Baldwin Theatre date.

Watching Adam appease his hunger increased her own. The icebox yielded cheese, fruit, and milk; a tin of sardines completed her meal. Sated, she went into her sitting room. Cold air trickled in around the window frame, and she made a mental note to ask the building's owner to have it recaulked. No, better make it a written note: There were too many other things on her mind to trust memory alone. She used a tablet and pencil on the side table, then turned up the gas fire and sat in her favorite Morris chair, curling up under an afghan that had been crocheted by one of Stephen's three aunts in Missouri whose names she could never keep straight.

Her thoughts shuttled back and forth between the Blanchford case and the perplexing business with Carson and the crackbrain Sherlock. But there was nothing definite to be concluded about either matter until she had gathered more information. Now that Andrea Scarlett was in safe hands, she could devote all of tomorrow to that goal.

After a while the combination of full stomach and warm fire made her drowsy. She was on the edge of falling asleep when her front door buzzer sounded. The sudden ratchety noise jerked her upright in the chair. Blinking, she peered at the Ansonia clock on the mantelpiece. It read 8:20. Who would be calling at this hour?

It turned out to be a uniformed young man from one of the messenger services. She felt a nasty sense of foreboding as she accepted the sealed message, but when she opened the envelope what she found was merely perplexing and not a little irritating.

My dear Mrs. Carpenter:
We must speak in person tonight on a most ticklish matter. I am sure you are aware of the Crocker Spite Fence in Huntington Park, Nob Hill. I will await your arrival no later than 10 P.M. You will, I believe, find our colloquy most interesting.

Your obedient servant,
SH, Esq.

The aggravating Mr. Holmes. But if he wanted to speak to her, why hadn't he simply called on her here? Why send a cryptic message? And what did "ticklish matter" mean? It smacked of one of his typically annoying melodramatic gambits, like the assuming of outlandish disguises for no sensible purpose. He never did anything in a normal, straightforward fashion — one of the reasons John considered him a lunatic best confined to an institution.

The Crocker Spite Fence in Huntington Park. That was at the very top of Nob Hill, not far from the mansion built by Carson's father, Evander Montgomery, a prominent stockbroker, where Carson resided. Was that why Holmes had stationed himself in such a curious place after dark, to continue his shadowy watch on Carson? And was that why he wanted to see her, to impart information about his motives?

She would have to meet him, of course, even though it meant a pair of somewhat lengthy cab rides and a late hour before she finally went to bed. Whatever was on his skewed mind, she had nothing to fear from him; he may have been an addlepate, but judging by past experiences he was a benign one. Besides, Nob Hill was among the city's safest neighborhoods at any hour of the night. And Huntington Park, with its fountain and many trees, paths, and benches, was located more or less in the shadow of Grace Cathedral. If the good Lord couldn't protect her there, where could He?

Nevertheless, she made sure the pearl-handled Remington derringer she kept in her bag was fully loaded before she left her rooms.

The chilly hansom ride to Nob Hill increased her agitation toward the crafty Mr. Holmes. She was in no mood for any more of his silly games when the cab arrived at their destination. She asked the driver to wait for her, and when he asked for payment in advance before agreeing, her irritation rose another notch. Did she look dowdy enough not to belong in the rarefied atmosphere of Nob Hill?

Now where did that thought come from? I'm not dowdy! I dress well, even if Callie says my wardrobe could do with a little pick-me-up. . . .

Sabina ventured along the graveled walk into Huntington Park, her high-button shoes whispering through a carpet of fallen autumn leaves. The charming little park, with its newly installed electroliers, appeared deserted at this hour. There was no sign of Holmes as she walked uphill toward the spite fence.

The unattractive fence, well-known among city residents, was a monument to greed and belligerence. After railroad magnate

Charles Crocker had purchased the top of Nob Hill in the mid-eighteen-seventies, he discovered that he had neglected one small parcel — a patch of land belonging to prominent undertaker Nicholas Yung. When Yung refused to sell the parcel for what Crocker considered a fair price, the tycoon contrived to drive him out of his home by erecting a high wooden fence that blocked out most of the light and views. To Yung's credit, he and his family continued thereafter to refuse all of Crocker's subsequent offers of purchase. His wife, Rosina, had a considerable estate of her own, and had been quoted in one of the newspapers as stating that the Yungs "took great pleasure in keeping our lot from the grasping hands of that dreadful old greed merchant."

The night was quiet here, the only sounds those of distant carriage wheels rumbling on cobblestones and water splashing musically in the fountain. Except for the pale glow of the scattered electroliers, the trees and shrubbery were shrouded in shadow. Lights outlined the towers of Grace Cathedral at the far end, and windows in the elegant homes that surrounded the park. One of the nearby homes, she knew, was the Montgomery mansion where Carson resided.

She reached the fence, still without seeing any sign of her annoying summoner, and moved along its perimeter. One of the little benches was set under a tree near where another path diverged from the one she was on. As she passed it, a dark shape suddenly materialized from behind the tree, stepping out in front of her. Startled, her hand darted inside her bag to touch the derringer's handle.

But of course it was only the would-be Sherlock Holmes. He swept off a top hat, bowed, and said, "Good evening, Mrs. Carpenter," in his familiar, British-accented voice. "How lovely to share your company again, even under difficult circumstances."

"Bah," Sabina said angrily, using one of John's favorite expressions to tell Holmes how *un*lovely it was to share his company again. Not that it fazed him in the slightest. "Did you have to jump out of the shadows like a footpad?"

"My apologies, dear lady. A small lapse in judgment. Apologies as well for requesting a meeting at such an unconventional place and time."

"Then why did you? Why didn't you simply call at my rooms like any normal person?"

"I am not a normal person," he said, a

151

statement with which Sabina agreed whole-heartedly. "I am Sherlock Holmes, as you well know, the world's greatest detective. No offense to you and your estimable partner, merely a simple declaration of fact."

"You didn't answer my question."

"Shall we sit down on yon bench to continue our discussion?"

He attempted to take her elbow, but she shrugged off his hand and went to seat herself without aid. He plopped down beside her at a respectful distance, holding his hat on one knee and his blackthorn walking stick upright alongside. The nearest electrolier was some distance away, so she couldn't see his face clearly. But she could make out that in addition to the top hat, he wore an unbuttoned great-coat that revealed striped trousers and a cutaway coat with a large white boutonniere. Not his usual attire, but also not one of his weird outfits, thank heaven; more or less appropriate attire for this exclusive neighborhood.

"You still haven't answered my question," she said. "Why didn't you call at my rooms instead of opting for melodrama?"

"Melodrama? *Mais non!* Decorum and necessity dictated our meeting here."

"What does that mean, exactly?"

"Decorum because I deem it unseemly

152

for a gentleman to visit a lady in her home after dark. Necessity because I am engaged in an investigation which requires my presence here until midnight at the very earliest."

"What sort of investigation?"

"I believe you have already deduced that it involves your swain, Carson Montgomery."

"Carson Montgomery is not my swain, merely a casual acquaintance." Sabina said this sharply and without hesitation. It was true, of course, but why had she been so abrupt in denying it?

She thought she saw the Englishman smile, though she couldn't be sure in the darkness. "As you wish," he said. "A matter of semantics, eh?"

"What is this 'investigation' of yours all about? Why did you summon me here?"

Instead of responding, Holmes in his unpredictable fashion commenced to sniff the air like an animal keening scent. "You have excellent taste in perfume," he said after a few seconds. "I detect attar of roses, orange blossoms, and gardenias. An interesting and unusual blend of fragrances. Distinctly Parisian. Marquis St. Germain number three, is it not?"

Sabina had long ago ceased to be surprised by one of Holmes's irrelevant observations; they were invariably and uncannily correct, which made them even more exasperating. The expensive French perfume, only a tiny dab of which she wore, had been a gift from Callie last Christmas.

Before she could speak, the Englishman sniffed again and then declared, "Ah, green apple, pilchards of the herring family Clupeidae, and the American version of bleu de Gex, an adequate *fromage* though of course vastly inferior to our English Stilton. I trust you enjoyed your simple evening meal, dear lady."

"Such delicate nostrils you have," Sabina said acidly.

"Indeed. My olfactory sense is almost as well developed as my powers of observation and ratiocination —"

"Why are you investigating Carson Montgomery?"

"At this point in time I am not at liberty to reveal the exact nature of my inquiries. Suffice it to say that the matter is well in hand and Mr. Montgomery appears to be in no imminent danger."

Sabina seldom lost her temper. When she did, it was exactly opposite of the way in which John lost his; instead of explosively fulminating, she became as cold and hard as a block of ice. "Mr. Holmes," she said in frigid tones, "have you ever been shot?"

"I beg your pardon?"

"Shot. Had a portion of your anatomy perforated with a bullet."

"No, although I once suffered a painful knife wound during the course of one of my adventures. And I have on occasion been forced to use my Webley Bulldog pistol in self-defense. Why do you ask?"

"Because you're about to be if you don't stop dithering and answer my questions."

"Dear me. Would you really shoot me with the Remington double-barrel derringer you carry in your handbag?"

"I might very well —" Sabina broke off abruptly. "How do you know the type of weapon I carry? Or that I carry one at all? I've never drawn it in your presence."

"I know many things, as you are quite well aware. Yes, indeed. Many, many things."

"*Are* you going to explain yourself? I warn you, you've sorely tried my patience and I am not a woman to be trifled with."

"I never for a moment believed you were. I certainly have no intention of trifling with you, or incurring your wrath to the point of violence."

"Well, then?"

"I requested this meeting because of your

association with Carson Montgomery. I was not aware of your unfortunate liaison with him until I saw you dining together at the Palace of Art restaurant."

"Unfortunate? Why did you use that word?"

"I consider you a friend as well as a colleague," the Englishman said. "It would distress me if you were to be placed in difficult circumstances."

"What do you mean by that?"

"Should you become more deeply involved with Mr. Montgomery."

"That's an evasive answer. Are you trying to tell me he's in some kind of trouble?"

"Such a conclusion may be drawn, yes."

"And that he's a criminal?"

"I made no such allegation."

"You implied it," Sabina said. "It's a preposterous notion. Carson Montgomery is a paragon of respectability."

"None of us is a true paragon, Mrs. Carpenter. We all have secrets, shameful fragments of our past that make us susceptible."

"Susceptible to what?"

"The acts of other, unscrupulous individuals. Extortion and blackmail, for instance."

"Now what are you saying? That Carson

is being blackmailed over something in his past?"

"Do you find that beyond the realm of possibility?"

"For heaven's sake, stop being so mysterious! If he is the victim of blackmail, why and by whom?"

"As I told you, I am not at liberty to divulge the details of my inquiries. However . . ." Holmes paused. "Are you familiar with the Gold King scandal of several years ago?"

"No. I've never heard of it."

"Then the name Artemas Sneed is likewise unfamiliar."

"Completely. Who is he? What is the Gold King scandal?"

"A competent detective such as yourself will surely be able to find out and proceed accordingly."

"Why can't you simply tell me yourself?"

Just then the cathedral bells tolled the hour. Holmes stirred on the bench, clamped the top hat firmly on his narrow skull, and rose to his feet so quickly it was almost a jump. "Ten o'clock," he said. "I must be off."

"Wait! We haven't finished —"

"Ah, but we have. I mustn't tarry; more of the game may be afoot tonight. *Bonne chance,* dear lady."

And he was off, moving with surprising speed and agility into the shadows. Sabina briefly considered trying to follow him, but as elusive as he was, and with her clothing hindering her own movements, she had little chance of keeping him in sight. And even if she caught up with him, he wouldn't tell her any more than he already had.

She made her way back through the park to the waiting hansom, concern vying with anger and bewilderment. Hidden secrets. Blackmail. Something called the Gold King scandal. Whatever all of that had to do with Carson she meant to waste no time in finding out.

Competent detective, indeed!

12

QUINCANNON

During his years as a Secret Service agent and subsequently as a private investigator, Quincannon had developed contacts with an array of individuals on both sides of the law. The one he counted on most was Ezra Bluefield, the owner of a Barbary Coast deadfall called the Scarlet Lady, but Bluefield's influence and knowledge didn't extend to Chinatown. Nor did that of any of the shady characters who were constantly on the earie for bits and pieces of information to sell. And since he himself had had little enough involvement in Chinatown affairs until the present Scarlett case, he knew no one within that close-knit, stoic community whom he could approach directly for the address of James Scarlett's lady friend, Dongmei.

His only alternative, then, was another evening's prowl through Chinatown, this time in the sections in which the area's multitude of bagnios flourished. Even with the lingering threat of tong violence, white men bent on amorous adventure in Oriental parlor houses and cribs, like those foolishly bent on gambling and whoring in the dangerous Barbary Coast, would be in sufficient enough supply so that he would not attract attention. The right amount of money could buy anything from the flower willows and madams, including the type of information he sought.

There were dozens of cribs on Jackson and Washington Streets, and in Bartlett, Brooklyn, China, and other dingy alleys throughout the Quarter. Most were small, crowded one-story shacks that catered to men of all races, occupied by girls who spoke no more English than the sly come-ons they'd been taught: "China girl nice! You come inside, please? Your father, he just go out!" Quincannon avoided these. None of the crib girls was likely to know where a courtesan of some standing resided alone. A much better bet was one of the parlor houses that catered to wealthier customers.

These were reputed to be lavishly furnished establishments staffed by attractive tarts richly dressed, seductively perfumed, and often quite young. The first one he entered, on Waverly Place shortly past seven-thirty, lived up to that reputation. But it was also one of the smaller houses, with four to six flower willows, all of whom were busy, as early as it was; two men awaited their turns in the incense-clouded parlor. When the middle-aged Chinese madam refused to talk to him, he tried casually questioning the men. That bought him nothing but head shakes and muttered negatives.

His luck was no better at the next parlor house he visited, nor at any of the half-dozen others large and small on Waverly and in Ross Alley that followed. None of the women or their clientele knew or admitted to knowing Dongmei. By the time he left the last of these "palaces of joy," he was beginning to think, ruefully, that he'd erred in assuming James Scarlett's mysterious lady friend was a courtesan.

Who and what was she, then? Not a shopgirl or other woman of lower caste, certainly. In order to afford the luxury of living alone, she would have to be the daughter or mistress of a highborn and influential Chinese. Mayhap one of the elders in the Hip Sing Company? That not only seemed possible but likely. If it was Dongmei who had started Scarlett on his opium addiction, as their client had suggested to Sabina, it might well have been at the behest of Bing Ah Kee, or Mock Don Yuen, or Mock Quan, in order to entice the attorney into providing his legal services to the tong.

Well and good, if this reasoning was correct. Find Dongmei and more than just the whereabouts of Scarlett's private papers stood to be learned. But finding her was still the problem. How to go about it now?

One possibility was Police Lieutenant William Price. As head of the Chinatown Squad, the "American Terror" had files on members of all those engaged in smuggling, gambling, and other criminal activities. If Dongmei was in fact related to one of the Hip Sing leaders, information about her might well be included in the Hip Sing file.

On the chance that Price might still be found at the Hall of Justice, Quincannon made his way there by trolley car and shank's mare. The effort paid dividends; the lieutenant was in fact still on duty, he was told at the front desk, and could be found in the basement assembly room. This was where the booking station and the odious cells of the city prison were located. He jostled through the usual crowded mix of coppers, handcuffed prisoners, attorneys, and bail bondsmen and entered the assembly room.

Here he not only found Price but evidence that the Chinatown flying squad was being mobilized. The room was strewn with coils of rope, firemen's axes, sledgehammers, artillery, and bulletproof vests similar to the coats of chain mail worn by the *boo how doy.*

"What's all this?" he asked the lieutenant. "Preparations for a raid on Chinatown?"

"Preparations only, for now. Tomorrow . . ." Price shrugged wearily. He looked as if he hadn't been to bed since their last meeting, which was probably the case. The fact that he'd nibbled a corner of his mustache into a ragged line indicated how worried he was. "Chief Crowley's orders."

"I thought it was settled that the strategy was to wait before sending out the flying squad."

"It was and should continue to be, as far as I'm concerned. But Gentry is still pressing for a raid on Little Pete's shoe factory. The mayor's office, too — demands for action, as if that would prevent rather than trigger a tong war. The chief hasn't given in yet, but the order to begin mobilizing indicates which way he's leaning."

"There's nothing you can do?"

"Not tonight. He's gone to consult with Mayor Sutro. I'll have another talk with him in the morning, but unless there are new developments between now and then I expect to be overruled." Price scrubbed a hand over his craggy face, pinched at the bags under bloodshot eyes. "What brings you here this time of night, Quincannon? I don't suppose you've found out anything pertinent or you'd have said so by now."

"Nothing worth sharing just yet," Quincannon hedged. "I was hoping for a look at your file on the Hip Sing."

"Why?"

"To see if there is anything that might help explain Scarlett's murder."

"There isn't. I'd have spied it myself if there was."

"I'd appreciate a look anyway."

"Reaching for straws? Your own investigation at a dead end?"

"Only for the time being."

Price considered, chewing at the ragged corner of his mustache. At length he said, "Ordinarily I wouldn't allow an outsider access to my files. But you're no run-of-the-mill flycop, you've been square with us so far, and you do have a vested interest in this business. Do I still have your promise to turn over anything important you might learn?"

"You do."

"Immediately?"

"Immediately." A stretching of the truth, perhaps, but not an outright lie.

"Very well, then."

They rode the elevator upstairs to Price's small, cluttered office. His Chinatown files were in a locked steel cabinet; he opened it with one of the keys on his watch chain, removed the Hip Sing file, relocked the cabinet, and sat down behind his desk before relinquishing the thick accordion folder. He kept a watchful eye as Quincannon paged through the various dossiers, reports, and other papers. Like all policemen, his trust of nonmembers of the force extended only so far.

It was in the Mock Quan dossier that Dongmei's name first appeared. She was indeed the daughter of a highborn Chinese, Wong Fu, one of the Hip Sing elders, and a known consort of Mock Don Yuen's rascally son. Quincannon then found a separate, single-page dossier bearing her name. It gave her age as twenty-two, yielded a Clay Street residence address, and offered an unsubstantiated opinion that her favors were granted to men in a position to benefit the Hip Sing. He scanned through a sheaf of arrest records, all of the names evidently those of highbinders and other low-level tong members. Dongmei's was not among them. Nor were Mock Quan's or Mock Don Yuen's.

The last of the dossiers he examined pertained to James Scarlett's legal manipulations for the tong. It told him nothing he didn't already know. Dongmei's name was not mentioned there, either.

"Well, Quincannon?" Price asked when he closed the file and handed it back across the desk.

He had assumed a frustrated expression while reading and now allowed it to deepen. "Nothing enlightening, I'm sorry to say."

"Everything in this file is strictly confidential. You'll remember that, I trust?"

"Of course, Lieutenant. You have my word on it."

"Beat it, then. I still have a report to write before I can put an end to this long damned day."

Outside in the misty darkness, Quincannon considered the advisability of returning to Chinatown to call on Dongmei tonight. And decided against it. The hour was late and it was likely she would refuse to open her door to a stranger . . . if in fact he was a stranger to her. He stood a better chance of gaining an audience come morning.

Despite the potential flying squad raid on

the morrow, he was in reasonably good spirits as he headed home. His day, despite its drawbacks, had been more productive by far than Price's. The connections between Dongmei and James Scarlett, Dongmei and Mock Quan, indicated he was on the right track. It seemed even more likely now that Mock Quan had had one hand, if not both, in the Chinatown intrigue. What was still unclear was the motive for Scarlett's murder, the extent (if any) of Mock Don Yuen's involvement, and the significance (if any) of "blue shadow" and Fowler Alley. There were other murky factors still to be clarified as well, among them whether or not he, too, had been an intentional target of the ambush outside the Cellar of Dreams.

Ah, but it was only a matter of time now until all became clear. He could feel it in his bones. When one of John Frederick Quincannon's investigations reached such a certain point, as this one had, a successful outcome was quite literally money in the bank.

13
SABINA

Sabina didn't sleep long or well that night. Too many things weighing on her mind, made even more acute by the odd and disturbing meeting with the would-be Sherlock Holmes. She disliked using makeup as so many other modern women now did, but the dark circles under her eyes required an application of powder and a touch of Pan-Cake. Adam gobbled his breakfast before streaking for the window she left partially open for him to come and go, but she had little appetite herself — a certain sign that she was out of sorts. But her determination to get to the bottom of the Blanchford case and the situation with Carson and the English poseur's insinuations about him hadn't waned; if anything, it was even stronger this morning.

Before going downtown to hunt the additional information she needed, she felt obligated to stop at Elizabeth Petrie's flat to see how Andrea Scarlett was faring. Much better, it seemed; Elizabeth had taken her well in hand, and the ex-police matron's strong, motherly influence had eased her fears considerably. The two women had struck up a bond over their shared interest in needlecraft, as Sabina had hoped they might. Elizabeth was teaching her charge some new sort of stitch whose intricacies went well beyond Sabina's limited knowledge of sewing. Fortunately, her upbringing, though it had emphasized the usual woman's homemaking role, hadn't excluded a broader, more sophisticated education.

Once downtown, her first stop was the building on Commercial Street that housed the *Morning Call.* Founded in 1856, it was generally the least guilty of the city's sheets of inflammatory yellow journalism, and often ran articles on such topics dear to Sabina's heart as the abuses of women. Still, it was not altogether a paragon, on occasion joining the *Examiner* and others in reporting drunken escapades, sexual misconduct, political hijinks, and the alleged evils of the "heathen Chinee." One of the two employees she'd come to see, society editor Millie Munson, with whom she'd formed a friendly relationship, was not at her desk. She was due back shortly, however, Sabina was told.

The other casual acquaintance was present — Ephraim Ballard, the old man in a green eyeshade who presided over the *Call*'s morgue. Despite his age, Ballard's memory was both prodigious and reliable. "The Gold King scandal?" he said in answer to Sabina's question. "Why, sure, I recollect it. Mostly happened in Amador County . . . let's see, about eight years ago. Had to do with the high grading of gold ore. You know what that is, high grading?"

"Yes. Was the story well covered in the *Call*?"

"It was, on account of a local bigwig being mixed up in it."

"Do you remember his name?"

"Kinney. George M. Kinney. An investor and former Gold King Mine stockholder who'd fallen on hard times."

The name was unfamiliar, thankfully. "I'd appreciate it if I could look at the requisite back issues."

"No sooner asked than done."

It took Mr. Ballard only a short time to locate the issues. The first one, dated July 11, 1887, broke the story under bold black headlines.

GOLD THIEVES UNMASKED
Half a Million Dollars Stolen from Gold King Mine
Prominent Local Investor Among Dozen
Implicated in High Grading Scheme

Sabina read quickly through the list of names of the other men involved. Artemas Sneed, a foreman at the mine, had been a ringleader along with the local investor, George M. Kinney, who was believed to have masterminded the scheme. The mine owners and the authorities had been alerted by an anonymous letter from a dutiful if diffident citizen who had stumbled on the high grading by accident, and the subsequent roundup of gang members had been rapid and sweeping.

Theft was a constant problem in the gold-mining industry, the account stated, though never before on such a large organized scale as this, for the Gold King Mine had been a multimillion-dollar producer of gold, one of the largest in the Mother Lode, employing hundreds of workers. The thieves had not resorted to the most common method of removing stolen high grade from the depths of the mine — the concealment of chunks of gold-rich ore inside lunch pails, double or false-crowned hats, long socks or cloth tubes hung inside trouser legs, and/or pockets sewn into canvas corset covers worn beneath the shirt. Rather they had used tube mills, short lengths of capped iron pipe with a bolt for a pestle, to pulverize chunks of rich ore into gold dust, which was much easier to smuggle out.

Subsequent issues carried more details about the high-grading operation, the recovery of some of the stolen gold, and the individuals involved. The trials in Amador County were covered in detail, the convictions and sentences imposed on the gang members ballyhooed as examples of swift criminal justice. George M. Kinney and Artemas Sneed received the stiffest prison terms, ten years in San Quentin each.

When Sabina finished reading, she sat thinking for a time. Although Carson Montgomery's name had appeared nowhere in any of the news stories, could he still have been involved and somehow escaped the fate of the others? By his own admission he'd roamed the Mother Lode during the 1880s, plying his trade in mines in several counties; the Gold King Mine in Amador could have been among them. And there was his reticence in talking about that period in his past. Yet she had a difficult time envisioning a man of his wealthy family background joining a gang of gold thieves . . . unless he'd been forced into it for some reason. And why had the bughouse Sherlock specifically mentioned Artemas Sneed, out of all the other known gang members?

She asked Mr. Ballard about Sneed, but he knew nothing of the man beyond his part in the high-grading operation. Which meant, given his infallible memory, that Sneed's name had not been mentioned in the *Call* since 1887. He did recall that George M. Kinney's health had failed rapidly after his incarceration and that he'd died in prison of pneumonia in 1892.

Puzzling and disturbing, all of this, to say the least.

Millie Munson was at her desk when Sabina returned to the city room. She was a tall, thin, rather plain woman who looked more like the popular conception of a schoolmarm than a society editor — a position she hated, but worked at diligently because it was one of the few opportunities for a woman journalist. In private, she had once referred to herself as "a semirefined upstart from the Arizona desert who can shoot the eye out of a rattlesnake at fifty paces." She was also an excellent observer who seemingly knew everything that went on among the city's upper echelons, and not above gossiping about it.

"What brings you here?" she asked, drawing Sabina to the chair beside her desk. Her brown eyes twinkled. "It wouldn't be to make an announcement, I suppose?"

"Announcement?"

"About you and Carson Montgomery. My spies tell me you've been stepping out with him."

Sabina managed a smile. "We have only had a few dates, Millie. Our relationship hasn't gone beyond the casual stage."

"But it might yet, hmm? Carson would be quite a catch."

"I imagine he would." She chose her next words carefully. "He's not only handsome and well bred, but evidently a man of high moral character."

"That he is. Though I'm sure he, like most men, has done his share of wildcatting."

"But committed no blemishes on the family escutcheon?"

"Nary a one I'm aware of. If your feelings for him do lead to an engagement, you'll be sure to let me know right away so I can break the news in my column?"

"On my oath."

"Splendid! Now then, why have you come

174

to see me? Something to do with one of your investigations?"

"Yes. Of course I can't reveal the specific nature of the case, but it concerns one of the city's more prominent families, the Blanchfords."

"Oh? Some sort of financial matter?"

"Why do you say that?"

"Well, there have been rumors that Ruben Blanchford and his philanthropic foundation were no longer quite as solvent as they seemed before his death. You weren't aware of that?"

"No. I understood he left quite a large estate."

"Large enough, certainly," Millie said, "but Ruben was generous to a fault in funding the foundation, and apparently none too wise when it came to recent stock market investments. The rumors hint at fairly substantial losses. Though if he hadn't become ill and died, he might well have recovered. You never see society gents in top hats standing in the bread lines, now do you?"

"Come to think of it, no. Nor society widows such as Harriet Blanchford. What's your opinion of her?"

"A rather headstrong woman, matriarchal, with conservative attitudes where money is concerned. She must not have been consulted when the bad investments were made. She'll make certain the balance of the family fortune remains intact."

"What about the son, Bertram? I understand he's a promoter of some sort."

Millie laughed, revealing her rather large teeth. "In his case 'promoter' is a polite term for dabbler in various not very lucrative enterprises, mainly those involving the so-called sport of kings."

"What else can you tell me about him?"

"Not very much, I'm afraid. He shuns the social scene so I've had virtually no contact with him. One of those feckless young men who drift through life with little or no purpose, tolerated because of their background but not held in high regard." Millie laughed again. "A bachelor not necessarily by choice, but because no self-respecting woman would have him."

Ross Cleghorne, self-styled "florist to the wealthy and influential," operated out of an elaborate shop on Geary Street. The fresh scents of myriad blooms and flowering plants enveloped Sabina as she entered, and she couldn't help but be impressed once again by the array of floral arrangements completed and awaiting pickup or delivery;

176

they were beautiful and original, with everyday items such as bits of metal, ribbons, fancy buttons, fragments of seashells, and oddly shaped and colored shards of glass nesting among the blossoms and greenery. Each of the various ornaments on display to complement his creations was also tastefully elegant.

Mr. Cleghorne was not a prepossessing figure, barely five feet tall and somewhat pear-shaped, but his effusive charm and impeccably tailored clothing more than made up for his lack of stature. To create the illusion of greater height, at least in his own mind, he wore his full head of white hair in an upswept pompadour and generous lifts in the heels of his patent-leather shoes. There was something endearing in his spritely salesmanship methods, at which he had few peers. They were on full display at the moment, as he succeeded in selling a well-dressed couple a rock-and-coral fountain for their daughter's wedding reception.

When the transaction ended and his customers departed, Mr. Cleghorne greeted Sabina effusively, bowing and taking both her hands in his. "My dear Mrs. Carpenter. To what do I owe this unexpected pleasure?"

"A small corsage of your choosing. And if you will, the answers to a few questions."

He smiled brightly. In addition to being an excellent florist, Ross Cleghorne, like Millie Munson, was not above discreetly telling tales about the city's elite as long as they wouldn't prove harmful to his business or his reputation. He had proven in the past to be an excellent source of information. But before he would impart anything, it was tacitly understood that a quid pro quo purchase had to be made. Hence Sabina's request for the corsage.

"I have the perfect confection for you already assembled," he said, beaming. "I shall fetch it once we've had our little talk." He drew her to a corner of the shop, out of hearing of his assistants at work in the large room behind the sales counter. "What is it you would like to ask me?"

"In the strictest confidence, Mr. Cleghorne."

"Of course, dear lady. I often indulge in a bit of gossip, but I never reveal a confidence when sworn to secrecy."

"It's about Carson Montgomery."

"Ah! The handsome and eligible Mr. Montgomery. You and he have been keeping company, I'm told."

Everyone seemed to know about her and Carson. Did that include John? If so, he had shown remarkable restraint in not confront-

178

ing her with the knowledge.

She repeated what she'd told Millie about the casual nature of the relationship. Then she asked, "How well do you know Carson?"

"Not well. A customer now and then. Pleasant chap, well mannered."

"He worked in the Mother Lode gold mines in the mid to late eighties. Do you know anything about that period in his life?"

Mr. Cleghorne considered, pinching his lower lip between thumb and forefinger. "No, I can't say I do."

"Or what prompted his decision to return to San Francisco?"

"A lucrative offer to join Monarch Engineering, I believe. And I imagine he'd had his fill of the rough-and-tumble life in the gold fields and decided it was time to settle down."

"When exactly was that, do you recall?"

"Oh, about eight years ago."

"In 1887, mid-year, perhaps?"

"Yes, I believe it was."

Sabina didn't pursue the subject any further. Mr. Cleghorne was incurably nosy and it wouldn't be wise to arouse his curiosity. He was a man of his word and would not intentionally break a confidence, but as much gossiping as he did, there was always the chance that he might let something slip to one of his customers. It wouldn't do for Carson to find out she'd been asking questions about him and his past. If he was innocent of any wrongdoing, and in no criminal danger despite the bughouse Sherlock's dire warning, she would surely continue to accept his social invitations.

She changed the subject to the Blanchford family. Mention of the name caused Mr. Cleghorne to make a little moue of dissatisfaction. "Yes, of course I know them. I had the privilege of creating several birthday and anniversary bouquets for Mrs. Harriet Blanchford at her husband's request. What I did not have the privilege of doing was handling the floral presentations for Mr. Blanchford's funeral."

"You weren't asked?"

"No. The honor went instead to the Fielder brothers, inferior florists if I do say so myself. I should have thought Mrs. Blanchford had better taste and a greater sense of loyalty. Either she was too distraught, or more likely, she allowed that gauche son of hers to make the arrangements. That would explain why the services were held in such an undesirable establishment as the Evergreen Chapel."

"You don't approve of Joshua Trilby?"

"Not in the least. Trilby is a second-rate mortician with a reputation for cutting corners and paying his bills only upon threat of legal action. If I *had* been asked to provide floral displays for Ruben Blanchford's funeral, I would have attempted to convince his widow to choose a more suitable venue. Otherwise I should have declined."

"Do you know Bertram very well?"

"I do not, nor do I want to." Mr. Cleghorne's moue grew even more pronounced. "Gentleman sportsman, my eye. The man is nothing but a common racetrack habitué. God only knows where he obtained the money to invest in the new Ingleside course."

Sabina knew about the new racetrack. The newspapers had run several stories about it since ground was broken in the sparsely populated Ingleside district southwest of downtown. The course was being constructed under the auspices of the Pacific Coast Jockey Club and would, according to one of the reports in the *Morning Call,* "inaugurate a new era of horse racing on this side of the continent." Construction of the track and a five-thousand-seat grandstand was nearing completion; its opening was scheduled for Thanksgiving Day, with quality breeders from all over the country shipping their horses to take part in the premier races.

"I didn't know Bertram was one of the investors," Sabina said.

"I have it on good authority that he is."

"Do you have any idea how much money he has in the project?"

"As much as he could scrape together, I suppose."

Another drain on the family finances?

There was nothing more to be learned from Ross Cleghorne. When Sabina had asked the last of her questions, he left her and soon returned with her corsage — a rather elaborate one consisting of a trio of white rosebuds, white Monte Casino, and variegated pittosporum laced with white ribbon. "And for you, Mrs. Carpenter," he said as he pinned it on her shirtwaist, "a special price of only ten dollars."

Only ten dollars!

Sabina had three more stops to make after leaving the florist shop. The first was at the offices of M. R. Wainwright & Associates, a financial consultancy firm whose advice and assistance she and John had sought in the past. There was little that Matthew Wainwright, its principal executive, did not know about the financial status of the city's prominent citizens. The fifteen minutes she spent with him turned out to be well worth her visit.

Slewfoot, the "blind" news vendor, and Madame Louella, a self-proclaimed Gypsy who told fortunes on Kearney Street at the edge of the Barbary Coast, were Sabina's two most reliable street informants. Both supplemented their incomes by gathering bits and pieces of salable information, much of it concerning illegal and quasi-legal activities in the Coast and other of the city's less desirable areas. But neither had anything worthwhile to tell her, at least not yet. They had never heard of Artemas Sneed or any sort of blackmail scheme involving what Sabina labeled "a member of the social elite," had no idea what the crackbrain Sherlock might be up to or where he was hanging his deerstalker cap, or knew anything about Bertram Blanchford or Joshua Trilby that she hadn't already been told.

Two dollars to each and the promise of more ensured that they would immediately spread the word among their many sources. If there was even the smallest piece of news to be learned, Slewfoot and/or Madame Louella would have it within twenty-four hours.

For the time being, then, all Sabina could do was wait.

14
QUINCANNON

The streets of Chinatown were even less populated today. The small number of black-clad, pigtailed men and work-stooped women abroad hurried on their errands, wariness in their movements, their usual singsong chatter muted. There was an almost palpable tension in the air. The danger of widespread tong violence, police raids, and vigilante retaliation from the Chinese-hating inhabitants of the poor white neighborhoods had spread fear throughout the Quarter.

Mock Don Yuen's herb shop was closed, shuttered, and apparently empty. Several sharp raps on the door and two more on the window glass brought no response. Well, this was no surprise. Whether or not the Hip Sing Company's new president was mixed up in the intrigue, he would be sensitive to the ominous rumblings and likely have sought refuge in the tong's headquarters.

Quincannon briefly considered another visit there and discarded the idea. Mock Don Yuen would surely refuse to see him, as would Mock Quan; chances were he wouldn't even be permitted to enter the building this time. There was nothing to be gained in making the effort. For that matter, he shouldn't have bothered coming here to the herb shop. Neither Mock Don Yuen nor anyone else in a position of power in Chinatown would have anything to say at this point to an Occidental detective with no official standing.

The Chinese woman, Dongmei, on the other hand . . .

The building in which she resided was on the steep section of Clay Street that rose above Portsmouth Square. Two stories, built of brick with a slatted wooden front, it stood between a pagoda-corniced temple and a larger structure that Quincannon guessed, by dint of its shuttered windows and profusion of Chinese characters, belonged to one of the small benevolent associations that dotted the Quarter. A balcony festooned with colored lanterns stretched across the upper floor; the windows behind it were likewise shuttered.

The entrance was narrow, recessed from the wooden sidewalk by two steps. The door there had no lock; it opened into a dark vestibule no larger than a cell. Stairs rose at its end, with another door behind them that would give access to the ground-floor apartment. Dongmei's would be the one upstairs, he judged, as befitted a woman of status in the community.

He climbed the stairs, quietly. The strong odor of incense came from behind the door on the landing above. He paused to listen, heard only silence, and rapped smartly on the panel, the sound echoing hollowly in the stillness. There was no response here, either.

Not that her apparent absence was necessarily disappointing. It might, in fact, be a blessing in disguise.

The door to her rooms was fitted with a locking plate, and when he tried the latch he found it secure. No locked door had ever deterred him for long, however, and this one was no exception. It took him less than thirty seconds of keyhole manipulation with the lock picks he carried, formerly the property of an East Bay scruff, to release the bolt.

Dongmei's abode, unquestionably. The unprepossessing building masked an apartment befitting the daughter of a highborn Chinese, a place as opulently furnished as any of the parlor houses. The furniture was of teakwood and bamboo, dominated by couches with soft cushions of embroidered silk; the walls were hung with exotic paintings, some of such an erotic nature that Quincannon couldn't help admiring them. Atop a wooden cabinet was a large bronze statue of Buddha. Elaborately painted screens and beaded curtains separated the parlor from other rooms, one containing an agreeably large canopied bed in a frame decorated with carved dragons. Brass and porcelain incense pots were the source of the heavy, still fresh scent that choked the air. Dongmei had not been gone for long.

He set about a rapid search of the premises. If Dongmei and Mock Quan *were* conjoined in the opium seduction of James Scarlett, it was highly doubtful that he would find the lawyer's private papers here. Anything of a sensitive nature that he might have left in her care would have been turned over to Mock Quan; might in fact have been the motive behind the assassination. What he did hope to find was evidence directly linking the pair to each other, if not to the late attorney.

There was nothing in the parlor that might have belonged to Scarlett or any other Occidental, or for that matter to a Chinese of

Mock Quan's Westernized tastes. None of the few handwritten documents tucked into a black-lacquered parlor cabinet were written in English.

Quincannon turned his attention to the bedroom. At the foot of the bed was a broad, intricately carved camphorwood chest. He unfastened the brass catch on the side of the chest, lifted the lid to look inside. Blankets. Silk sheets. An extra pillow. One of two bottom drawers contained several pieces of jade and ivory jewelry, valuable from the look of them, and little else. It was in the second that he found the first items of interest: a curved opium pipe, cooking bowl, needle, and a small supply of *ah pin vin.* Dongmei was either a hop smoker herself, or she kept the materials on hand for male callers such as James Scarlett and Mock Quan. Or perhaps both.

A dragon-decorated, red-and-black wardrobe contained several silk robes, two of them much larger than the others. Dongmei was obviously of a diminutive stature; the large robes were masculine attire, though their pockets contained nothing to indicate who had worn them. But as he was about to close the wardrobe doors, he spied the second item of interest on a corner shelf: a man's black slouch hat with a red topknot.

He was studying the hat, turning it in his hands, when the sound alerted him — that of a key scratching in the front door lock.

Caught, blast it! No sense in attempting to hide, even if the apartment had had a place large enough to conceal him. If the windows facing Clay Street had been un-shuttered, he might have managed to slip out onto the balcony and then to climb or drop down to the sidewalk. As it was, the only course of action open to him was to brazenly stonewall.

Quickly he replaced the hat, then hurried to the bead curtains and stepped through them into the parlor just as the door opened. The woman saw him immediately as she came inside; she stopped with the door still open, stood stock-still. Tiny she was, no more than five feet tall; shiny ebony hair hung in a long queue down her back, and what Quincannon imagined would be an enticing body was concealed inside a loose-fitting garment that covered her from head to foot. She was strikingly attractive, or would have been if her elfin features hadn't twisted into expressions of surprise and then cold fury.

"Fan kwei!" She spat the phrase at him.

Quincannon knew what it meant. *Fan kwei* — foreign devil. He assumed a sternly officious expression as he came forward, as if he had every right to be in her apartment.

Dongmei chattered at him briefly in Mandarin, with such vitriol that he had no doubt he was being roundly cursed. Then, abruptly, she switched to lightly accented English. "Why you break in here?" she demanded.

"Break in? The door was unlocked."

"You lie! Door locked like always. You steal something?"

"I'm not a thief."

"What you come here for?"

"Police business."

"Hai! You not police dog."

"No? Then who am I?"

"Quin-cannon." As if his name were two words instead of one, both of them obscene. "I know you."

"From Mock Quan, eh?"

She made the same kind of angry hissing sound Mock Quan had the day before. Then, "You go away now."

"Not until you tell me about Mock Quan and James Scarlett."

"I tell you nothing. Nothing!"

"Why was Scarlett killed?"

"Get out!"

"Talk to me or talk to the American Terror, Dongmei."

She made a spitting mouth, staring at him lynx-eyed, her hands hooked in front of her. The fingernails were an inch long and as sharp as claws. For a moment Quincannon thought that she might launch a furious attack, but when she moved it was away from him toward the windows.

She threw open the shutters, then the glass doors to the balcony. He knew what she was about to do then, even before she stepped out onto the balcony, but it was too late to stop her. She emitted an ear-piercing shriek, followed by a shrill string of Chinese words dripping with simulated terror and then more shrieks. Anyone on Clay Street below would think she was being raped or murdered and there would soon be a stampede, if not a riot.

Quincannon was no fool; he did the prudent if not the manly thing.

He fled.

A messenger service envelope was waiting for him when he returned to the agency — on the floor with the morning mail, having been pushed through the slot in the locked door. Sabina seemed not to have come in yet today. It must be that she was off investigating the Blanchford matter or perhaps another of her cases. The alternative, that she had spent a long, amorous, and exhausting night with the Montgomery swell, was too depressing to consider.

At his desk he sifted quickly through the mail, separating out the only piece which might contain a check for services rendered, but leaving it unopened for the moment. Then he gave his attention to the messenger service envelope.

As he'd anticipated, it was from Father O'Halloran's scholarly acquaintance, a man named Fosbury, and contained both the original two-page document from James Scarlett's office file and an English translation. He read and digested only a few sentences before putting it down. For the document was nothing more than a contract between Mock Don Yuen and the owner of the building in which he maintained his herbalist shop, extending a five-year lease for the shop and the rooms upstairs at no monthly increase.

The document made no mention of the fact that the upstairs rooms were being used for an illicit gambling operation, although the amount of money Mock Don Yuen was paying the owner indicated a percentage payoff. Even if the gambling had been mentioned, it had no direct bearing on Quincannon's investigation. The attorney, who had both spoken and read Chinese, must have acted as an intermediary in the financial negotiations between the two men and then vetted the agreement.

A waste of time and money, having the document translated? No. While it didn't absolve Mock Don Yuen of complicity in James Scarlett's murder, it strengthened Quincannon's growing belief that the old man was not the one plotting a criminal takeover of Chinatown. He was not cold-blooded enough, nor recklessly ambitious enough at his age, to have masterminded such a scheme. His son was. And so was Little Pete.

Which one, then? Or was it possible that the two of them were in cahoots, Mock Quan's vicious invective against Fong Ching nothing but a smokescreen? Possible, but highly unlikely. Pete had long been a ruling force in Chinatown crime, a man who relished his position of power; while he might want to gain command of the Hip Sing's gambling network, he would never agree to share with a rival to get it. If he was behind the Bing Ah Kee snatch, it was in an effort to gain control by devious means. Yet he had had plenty of opportunity to start war between the Kwong Dock and the Hip Sing before this, and hadn't done so. The death of Bing Ah Kee might have acted as a trigger; he could have other, hidden reasons as well. But it still seemed out of character for him to have risked the wrath of Blind Chris Buckley and the Chinatown flying squad by ordering the murder of a white man. Or, for that matter, to have made an ally of James Scarlett in the first place.

Which left Mock Quan. More and more, he seemed the most likely candidate. How to prove it, though? And how to do so before more blood was shed on the streets of Chinatown?

Quincannon sat staring into space, pondering the dilemma. He was still pondering, and beginning to make out the shape of things, when the sound of the door opening and Sabina's voice snapped him out of his reverie.

15
QUINCANNON

Sabina's demeanor immediately aroused Quincannon's suspicions. She looked less energetic than usual, sleep-deprived, and her "Good afternoon, John" had what he deemed a somewhat distracted, almost formal note. The result of a long, passionate night with that damned Montgomery fellow? The notion made his heart ache and his blood pressure rise.

It rose even higher when she shed her coat and he saw the white rose corsage pinned to the bosom of her shirtwaist. Before he could stop himself, he said, "That looks to be an expensive corsage. Where did you get it?"

"What would you say if I told you it was a gift from a secret admirer?"

"I'd ask you not to keep his name secret."

"Of course you would. Well, it wasn't. I bought it from Ross Cleghorne in exchange for some information. For ten dollars."

"Ten dollars! That coxcomb is as big a crook as some of those we've put in prison —"

"At least he's a gentleman most of the time."

Her snappish tone warned him that she was in no mood for any more personal questions or comments, and especially not badinage. (Not that he was in the mood for raillery, either.) Anything other than a strictly professional conversation would cause serious friction and that was to be avoided now more than ever.

"Was Cleghorne's information helpful to your investigation?" he asked.

"You mean the Blanchford case?"

"You have another at present?"

She was seated now at her desk, shuffling through the mail he'd placed there, and it seemed to him that she hesitated before answering. "No. Only my part in the Scarlett matter. I stopped at Elizabeth Petrie's earlier. She has Mrs. Scarlett's confidence as well as ours."

"Splendid."

"As for the Blanchford body snatching," Sabina said, "you needn't concern yourself. I have the matter well in hand." She didn't seem to want to discuss it in any detail. Playing her cards close to the vest, as he himself often did, until a resolution was imminent.

"I can say the same for the Scarlett affair. Though there are certain complications."

"Yes?"

He told her about his talk with Lieutenant Price the night before and the possibility of a premature raid on Little Pete's shoe factory. "It will serve no purpose except to turn up the heat on an already boiling pot. I doubt Fong Ching is behind the ferment in Chinatown. I'm more convinced than ever now that Mock Quan is the guilty party, working at cross-purposes to those of his father and the Hip Sing elders. But I don't have enough evidence to convince that blockhead Chief Crowley."

"What makes you so sure it's Mock Quan?"

"The nature of his character, or lack of it. He's capable of any vicious act, including cold-blooded murder. In fact, I'm beginning to believe that it was he, not one of the *boo how doy,* who shot James Scarlett."

Sabina arched a skeptical eyebrow. "Disguised as a coolie food seller? Why, for heaven's sake? Why wouldn't he have sent one of his hatchet men to do his dirty work?"

"I can't say for certain. He may have had

a personal reason. Or he may not have trusted an underling to break the Chinese code of non-violence against white men. Or it could be a mental aberration, a power-mad megalomaniac's need to indulge in daredevil acts and to satisfy bloodlust. He covets Little Pete's criminal empire, and he doesn't care a whit who dies, white or yellow, in his quest to take it over."

"You make him sound like a monster."

"Just so, if I'm right about him. And I believe I am."

"What led you to the conclusion he murdered Scarlett?"

"His hat."

"His — Are you serious, John?"

"Never more so. The gunman outside the Cellar of Dreams wore a black slouch hat with a dark-colored topknot, as I told you. The more I thought about that topknot, the more certain I became that its color was red. And a red topknot —"

"Is a symbol of the highborn."

"Yes. Exactly."

"It's called a *mow-yung,*" Sabina said.

Now it was Quincannon's turn for the lifting of an eyebrow. "How do you know its name?"

"And why shouldn't a woman know something you don't?"

He chose to let that pass without comment. "Coolie food sellers don't wear such hats and neither do the *boo how doy*. The assassin therefore has to have been a high-caste Chinese. To my knowledge Little Pete has never resorted to personal violence, and never against an Occidental. That leaves only Mock Quan."

"If it was a *mow-yung* on the shooter's hat."

"It was. I'm convinced of it."

"Mock Quan is just one of many highborn Chinese," Sabina pointed out.

"Yes, but he's the only one keeping company with the woman who seduced James Scarlett and started him on his opium addiction."

"Dongmei? You tracked her down?"

"I did. Last night I persuaded Lieutenant Price to allow me a look at his files. She's a known consort of Mock Quan's and her address was noted. I paid a visit to her apartment this morning."

"And what did she have to say for herself?"

"She wasn't there. I took advantage of the opportunity to search the premises."

"Illegal trespass, John?"

"In the cause of justice," he said piously. He saw no reason to mention his brief confrontation with Dongmei and its somewhat ignominious conclusion. "I found a black slouch hat with a red topknot among her effects. It could belong to no one except Mock Quan."

Sabina considered this. Then she asked, "What of the snatching of Bing Ah Kee's corpse? What is his purpose in that?"

"I'd bet five gold eagles," Quincannon said, "that he has the corpse stashed somewhere and intends to produce it soon, to be found somewhere that will place the onus on the Kwong Dock and bring about the tong war he desires. If that doesn't finish off Little Pete, he reckons, Will Price's flying squad will. Thus leaving him in a position to step into the wreckage and build a new criminal empire."

"Do you suppose he was intentionally trying to kill you, too, in Ross Alley?"

"I think so, yes."

"Because he recognized you, or with premeditation?"

"The former. It's unlikely he could have known I was searching for Scarlett that evening. I suspect he knew in which resort Scarlett was holed up, learned it from an informant perhaps, and went there with the intention of murdering him while he lay drugged inside. By happenstance I must have arrived just before he did. He recognized me, feared that Scarlett was my quarry as well as his and that the lawyer had told or would tell me something that might threaten his plans, and determined to kill me, too, if I emerged with Scarlett in tow, as I did. He set up his ambush by frightening off the genuine coolie food seller and assuming position over his brazier."

"And Fowler Alley?" Sabina said after a pause. "Have you learned its significance yet?"

"No, confound it. Although I feel as though I should have by now." He stood abruptly and went to the window overlooking Market Street, his hands clenched behind his back. Rumbling trolley cars and a near collision between one of them and a horse-drawn barouche held his attention for a few seconds. Then he turned and began to pace the office, muttering, "Fowler Alley, Fowler Alley . . ."

There was a sudden loud thumping on the office door. It brought him up short, and a second thump sent him to the door. When he opened it he found himself looking at an elderly woman dressed in black and wearing a black veil, a gold-headed walking stick upraised in one thin hand in preparation for a third thump.

"Yes, madam?"

"Are you the other half of Carpenter and Quincannon?"

"I am. John Quincannon, at your service. How may I help you?"

"By stepping aside and letting me enter. I've come to speak to Mrs. Carpenter."

"Is she expecting you?"

"No, but she will certainly see me. Well, young man?"

Quincannon stepped aside. Sabina was on her way around her desk, he saw out of the corner of his eye. The old woman entered and then stopped to lift her veil and scrutinize him as if sizing up a side of beef.

"He's a big one, isn't he," she said to Sabina.

"Yes, he is."

"Looks like pictures I've seen of Blackbeard, the scourge of the Spanish Main."

Quincannon wasn't sure whether to be flattered or offended until Sabina said, "John, this is our client Mrs. Harriet Blanchford." Then he allowed a bright professional smile to crease his whiskers.

"Ah, yes. A pleasure to meet you, Mrs. Blanchford, even under such trying circumstances —"

"Eyewash," the old lady said in her feisty way. "Whether or not it's a pleasure remains to be seen."

Sabina took gentle hold of her elbow, guided her to one of the client's chairs. "What brings you here?" she asked then. "Have you news?"

"I have. A decision that neither of you will agree with, I imagine, but that is neither here nor there. I've just come from my bank, the Whitburn Trust, where I made a substantial withdrawal of funds."

"You don't mean —"

"I do. For payment of the ransom demand."

16
SABINA

Sabina exchanged a look with John, whose smile had turned upside down. Before he could say anything, she asked Harriet Blanchford, "Tell us, please, why you decided to pay the ransom?"

"Bertram convinced me it had to be done," she said. "Another note was delivered this morning. Even more harshly worded and threatening than the first. It said my husband's remains would be . . . disposed of in a most disgusting fashion if the seventy-five thousand dollars wasn't paid this afternoon. The threat was too great to be ignored."

"Do you have the money with you?"

"No, Bertram has it. He is on his way to deliver it to the specified location."

"And that is?"

"Near one of the bandstands in Golden Gate Park."

Sabina repressed a sigh. As gently as she

could, she said, "I must say I wish you had consulted with me before withdrawing the funds."

"You would not have been able to talk me out of it. My mind was made up. Besides, there was no time for a consultation. The ransom is to be paid no later than four o'clock."

"One of us could have accompanied your son," John said, "perhaps apprehended the culprit —"

"I wouldn't have allowed it. It might well have jeopardized the safe return of my husband's remains. The note promised in its crude way that if instructions were followed to the letter, Ruben would soon be back in his final resting place."

"Unfortunately, the promises of kidnappers of any stripe are seldom to be trusted."

Sabina gave him a reproving look; he was not always as tactful as he should be. The old matriarch glared at him. "Are you saying these fiends *won't* keep their word?"

"Not at all," Sabina said quickly. "They may well return the body or inform you where it can be found."

"But it is a possibility I should be prepared for?"

"I'm afraid so. But even if that should be the case, it doesn't mean that any harm will have been done to the body. It might still be recovered intact."

"By whom? You? You have no idea who the kidnappers are or you would have said so by this time."

"That's not entirely true," Sabina said. "I am gathering information that I expect will soon reveal their identities."

"Indeed? What sort of information?"

"I would rather not say just yet."

"If you are being deliberately evasive, Mrs. Carpenter —"

"I assure you, I'm not. Merely cautious. You do want me to continue my investigation?"

"Naturally. I came here to keep you informed, not to discharge you. I want those fiends caught and punished for their heinous crime, whether they keep their promise or not."

"They will be," John put in. "And if at all possible, the seventy-five thousand dollars will be recovered and returned to you as well." Leave it to him to mention the money.

"That is the least of my concerns." With the aid of her cane, Harriet Blanchford rose to her feet. "I'll be going now. I want to be home when Bertram returns from the park."

"Please let us know right away of any new developments."

"I will."

John, in his courtly fashion, sought to take her arm as she started toward the door. She shrugged off his hand. "I am quite capable of making my own way, young man." She squinted up at him through her glasses. "You really ought to trim those whiskers of yours," she said then. "Blackbeard the pirate is one breed, Blackbeard the detective quite another."

Sabina hid a smile as the door clicked shut behind her. The expression on John's face was a delight to behold. He was not at all used to dealing with women of Harriet Blanchford's age and outspoken manner, and she'd left him more than a little nonplussed. Not that he would admit it. And of course he didn't.

John soon departed, not saying where he was bound for but only that he didn't expect to return before closing time. Alone in the quiet office, Sabina attended to necessary paperwork — reports, invoices — that had begun to pile up on her desk. While she worked, part of her mind reviewed the Blanchford case and what she'd discovered about the Gold King scandal.

The former was the least mystifying of the two. The fact that a second threatening note had convinced Harriet Blanchford to pay the ransom, she decided, was a blessing in disguise. Usually it was a bad idea to give in to the demands of kidnappers of the living or the dead, but in this case it might well hasten a successful conclusion. She was reasonably sure now that she knew the how, why, and who of the matter. By tomorrow, if the next development happened as she now anticipated, and if her informants came through with the necessary information she'd requested, she would know for certain and proceed accordingly.

The Gold King business was still a disturbing puzzle. Had Carson been mixed up with the high graders and somehow escaped being identified as one of the gang? Had Artemas Sneed been paroled from San Quentin, and was he in fact blackmailing Carson? And what, in the name of all that was holy, was the bughouse Sherlock up to? If only she could talk to him again! She would demand straightforward answers this time, if necessary at gunpoint. But of all the tasks she had set for Slewfoot, Madame Louella, and their coterie of sources, the present whereabouts of the elusive Mr. Holmes would likely prove the most difficult.

She mentally replayed her conversation

with Ross Cleghorne. He'd said that Carson had returned to San Francisco and taken a position with Monarch Engineering in the summer of 1887, the same month that the gold-stealing scheme had unraveled and the known gang members arrested. A coincidence? Or —

A sudden thought occurred to her. George M. Kinney, the man who had masterminded the gold-stealing plot, had been described by Ephraim Ballard as as an investor and former Gold King Mine stockholder. Had he been a client of Montgomery and DeSalle, Carson's father's brokerage firm? If so, it was quite possible Carson had known him. . . .

Ross Cleghorne might have the answer to that, but asking him any more questions might put him on alert. Who else could she consult? Ah, yes, Theodore Bonesall. The manager of Western States Bank, he was both a stock-market investor and a former client for whom she and John had successfully handled an embezzlement matter.

Western States Bank was on the Telephone Exchange. Sabina gave the operator the number, and after the usual delay in connecting and another as Mr. Bonesall was summoned to the telephone, she asked her carefully worded questions.

He had two pieces of information for her. The first answered her queries and unfortunately added to her doubts about Carson. Yes, Mr. Bonesall said, he'd known George M. Kinney moderately well before greed and poor investments had brought about the man's downfall. Kinney had in fact been a client of the Montgomery and DeSalle brokerage firm, and a close enough friend of Evander Montgomery that the latter reportedly had been badly shaken by the news of Kinney's arrest and conviction. That being the case, it was almost certain that Carson and Kinney had been acquainted, thus strengthening the likelihood of Carson's involvement in the gold-stealing operation.

The second piece of information, casually offered by Mr. Bonesall near the end of their conversation, was bemusing in a different way. For he asked if she was still keeping company with Carson Montgomery. How had he known she was? Well, as he'd told her partner, she and Carson had been seen dining together on two occasions, once by him and once by an acquaintance.

"You told this to Mr. Quincannon? Was he the one who brought up the subject?"

"No, I did. We met in passing and spent a

few minutes together over coffee. I happened to mention it to him, and I must say he was keenly interested. Shouldn't I have?"

She wanted to say, "No, you shouldn't. My personal life is of no concern to anyone but me." But it wouldn't do to take a sharp tone with a former client who had been cooperative and might require the agency's services again. She settled for saying, "It's of no consequence, Mr. Bonesall. Thank you again for your time and your candor."

So John *was* aware of her liaison with Carson. Knowing John and how he felt about her, "keenly interested" was an understatement. More likely he had been and still was acutely jealous. And no doubt he considered the relationship to be much more intimate than it was, imagining all sorts of lewd goings-on between her and the suave Mr. Montgomery. Why hadn't he said anything to her? Sneakily checking up on her and Carson? She wouldn't put it past him. Well, as long as he kept quiet, so would she. Let him stew in his own masculine juices. It served him right.

Sabina was just finishing up the paperwork when the young man arrived with an envelope clutched in one grubby hand. She knew him: a young half-wit named Cheney who acted as a runner and errand boy for several individuals, Madame Louella among them. He handed her the envelope without speaking, grinned foolishly when she gave him a quarter in exchange, and left her alone again.

The sheet of notepaper inside the envelope bore a single line of writing in a flowing hand.

Whereabouts A.S. known to me by 7 P.M.

Madame L.

A.S. — Artemas Sneed. The Gypsy fortune-teller had outdone herself; Sabina hadn't expected to hear from one of her informants so soon. Very fast service, indeed.

The Seth Thomas clock on the wall read 4:55 as Sabina pinned on her straw boater, donned her cape, and left the office. She had just enough time for an early, leisurely meal at Darnell's, one of the small restaurants near Union Square she favored, before once more venturing to Madame Louella's abode on Kearney Street. Despite another long day and the grim nature of the situation with Carson, she hadn't lost her appetite: She was, in fact, famished.

17
QUINCANNON

No sooner had he emerged from the building that housed Carpenter and Quincannon, Professional Detective Services, than he was accosted by Homer Keeps. The flatulent little muckraker for the *Evening Bulletin* had an air of sweaty eagerness, his puffy cheeks glistening in spite of the coolness of the afternoon. In the pocket of his cigar-ash-spotted coat he carried a folded copy of what was probably the latest edition of the rag that employed him.

"Ah, finally," he said. He removed the derby from his bald head, with its scraggly fringe of brown hair, and used it to fan himself as he spoke. "You're a difficult man to track down, sir."

Quincannon's desire to do Keeps bodily harm had cooled somewhat, though his fingers flexed and his palms itched at the man's nearness. He said, "And you're a difficult one to avoid," and kept on walking down Market Street.

Keeps scurried after him, caught his arm. This brought him once more to a halt, and earned the reporter a sharp swat on the knuckles. "Hands off, you little toad."

"Now, now." The reporter sounded aggrieved, but there was malice in his subsequent grin — one which revealed large nicotine-stained teeth any horse in the city would have been ashamed to own. "I merely took hold of your sleeve. I could press charges for assault, you know," he said, rubbing his knuckles. "And sue you for slander for the name you called me."

"You wouldn't dare do either. You use a pen filled with poisonous lies and innuendo to do your dirty work."

"I write the truth as I see it."

"Bah. Go away and stay away, Keeps. I have nothing to say to you." He began walking again.

The little muckraker hurried to keep pace. "What are you trying to hide, Mr. Quincannon?"

"From you, anything and everything."

"In particular the nature of your involvement in the Chinatown shooting, eh?"

"Bah," Quincannon said again. "I tried to prevent the death of James Scarlett while acting on behalf of a client. I was almost shot and killed myself, as you no doubt know."

"So you say. But is that the true version of what happened in Ross Alley?"

"It is, no matter how you try to twist it otherwise."

Keeps showed his equine teeth again. "Mrs. Andrea Scarlett is your client, is she not? What have you done with her?"

"Done with her? What kind of question is that?"

"She's nowhere to be found. Hiding her for some reason, are you?"

"If I were, which I'm not, I wouldn't admit it to the likes of you."

"What's your connection with the China-man known as Little Pete?"

"None whatsoever. Why mention his name?"

"We both know he is behind the theft of Bing Ah Kee's corpse."

"Do we? I'm sure I *don't* know it."

"The police think he is," Keeps said. "Why else would the Chinatown squad have raided Little Pete's shoe factory today?"

Quincannon scowled. "What's that?"

"Don't tell me you don't know about the noon-hour raid."

"I will tell you that because it's the truth. But I won't ask you for the details; you'd only distort them."

"Read all about it in the latest edition of the *Bulletin*. I was fortunate enough to finish my bylined account just before deadline."

Keeps tried to hand over the folded newspaper; Quincannon refused to take it. "My reading habits don't include trash."

The comment warped Keeps's mouth into petulant lines. He produced a small notebook and began to scribble in it, muttering, "Private detective refuses to answer questions pertaining to attorney's murder and raid on shoe factory, or his involvement with the heathen Chinee . . . caugghh!"

The last utterance, a crowlike squawk, was the result of Quincannon taking hold of his throat in one splay-fingered hand. He didn't squeeze as hard as he would have liked, barely squeezed at all as a matter of fact. But the grip was strong enough so that Keeps dropped the notebook and fumbled with both hands in a futile attempt to break free. A passing pedestrian, witnessing this, detoured widely around the two men.

"Now you have genuine cause to charge me with assault," Quincannon said menacingly. "But you won't do that, will you?"

"Caugghh."

"Nor will you publish any more vicious

lies about me. Not if you value what's left of your miserable life." He relaxed his grip and then removed his hand. "Well? Do we understand each other?"

Either Keeps had nothing to say or he had temporarily lost the power of speech. What he saw in Quincannon's face caused his eyes to bulge even wider; he bent swiftly to retrieve his notebook, spun on his heel, and went scuttling away, casting several backward glances as if he were afraid of being chased.

The Hall of Justice was quiet in the aftermath of the raid on Little Pete's factory. A small clutch of newshounds lurked in the vicinity of the front desk; Quincannon managed to avoid two of them, curtly refused comment when a third attempted to buttonhole him, and hurried upstairs to the detective division.

Lieutenant Price was present but away from his office. Quincannon sat on a bench outside the slatted room divider and waited with as much patience as he could muster. He smoked one bowlful of shag and was halfway through another when Price finally returned.

The American Terror looked like nothing of the sort. He appeared even more frazzled today, the luggage beneath his eyes larger and darker, both corners of his mustache now chewed into raggedness. He was not overjoyed to find Quincannon waiting for him.

"You wouldn't be here because you have information for me, I suppose?"

Quincannon was not ready to share his suspicions about Mock Quan, and wouldn't until he was able to back them up. He shook his head.

"Because of the raid this noon, then."

"I just learned of it, yes."

Price sighed heavily. "Well, all right, come into my office. I'll give you five minutes."

Once they were seated in the small, cluttered office, Price rubbed his tired eyes and gnawed a few more hairs off his mustache before he spoke. "There being no new developments overnight, Chief Crowley decided we'd waited long enough. I tried to talk him out of it but once his mind is made up . . ."

"Did you lead the raid?"

"Yes. Better me than Sergeant Gentry. I don't mind saying he's a hothead. If he'd had his way, there likely would've been more violence than there was."

"How much was there?"

"One man dead," Price said bleakly. "One

of Pete's bodyguards drew a knife and Gentry was forced to shoot him in self-defense. Unfortunately in one sense, perhaps fortunately in another."

"How do you mean?"

"The highbinder had a letter in his possession bearing James Scarlett's letterhead and signature."

"Oh? What kind of letter?"

"One linking Scarlett and Fong Ching."

Quincannon scowled. "I find that hard to believe. If Scarlett was a traitor to the Hip Sing, why wasn't he shot by one of their hatchet men instead?"

"Working both ends against the middle, perhaps."

"Are you certain the letter is genuine?"

"It would seem to be."

"But you're not convinced?"

"No. Although I can't think of any plausible reason why it should have been faked."

Neither could Quincannon at the moment. But the piscine odor tickled his nostrils again. "If it is genuine," he said, "why would Little Pete's bodyguard have had it in his possession? Why not Pete himself? For that matter, why would it have been kept at all?"

"All questions without answers yet."

"What did Pete have to say?"

"He denied any knowledge of the letter, of course — loudly and indignantly proclaimed it a forgery. Denied any involvement with Scarlett whatsoever. He defied us to find any more such evidence on the premises or anywhere else in his domain."

"And you found none."

"We went over his office and the rest of the factory with a fine-tooth comb. His home as well. Not so much as a scrap tying him to Scarlett, or to indicate he was responsible for the Bing Ah Kee snatch."

"So you didn't take him into custody."

"No. Gentry argued that the letter was sufficient cause, but without additional evidence . . ." Price essayed a frustrated shrug.

"Have there been any repercussions from the raid?"

"Not as far as we know. The sergeant was all for raiding Kwong Dock headquarters, too, but I quashed that notion. It would have been incendiary as well as another waste of time."

"The pot's bubbling hot enough as it is," Quincannon agreed.

"Close to boiling over is more like it." Price glanced at the Seth Thomas clock mounted on one wall. "Your five minutes are up."

Quincannon stood. "Before I go," he said, "would you allow me a look at the letter found on the dead bodyguard?"

"I might if I had it, but I don't. The chief took possession, and I'm not about to invade his office on your behalf."

"Would you at least tell me the gist of it?"

"It refers to payments allegedly made by Little Pete to Scarlett for inside information about Hip Sing activities. Amounts totaling nearly five thousand dollars." Price rubbed again at his bloodshot eyes. "On your way. And don't forget your promise to bring me anything pertinent you might come up with."

"I won't."

The letter was a forgery for sure, then, Quincannon thought as he left the lieutenant's office. Even an opium addict would not have been fool enough to commit to paper word of such underhanded dealings. But a forgery ordered by whom? Mock Quan?

No one else had passed through the portal marked J. H. SCARLETT, ATTORNEY-AT-LAW since Quincannon's nocturnal visit. Or if anyone had, it'd been without any further disturbance of the premises.

He set about once more sifting through

222

the dead lawyer's papers. His previous search had been as hasty as his predecessor's, and it was possible that they had both overlooked something of importance.

No, not a possibility but a fact, as he discovered when he carefully examined the documents pertaining to Scarlett's work for the Hip Sing. The hunch that bit him after several minutes of this had plenty of teeth: One name reappeared in similar context in several of the files, and the more he saw it, the more furiously his nimble brain clicked and whirred. When he stood at last from the desk, hunch had become certainty. He gathered the files together and tucked them under his arm. His smile and the oath he uttered through it had a wolfish satisfaction as he left the office.

He knew now most of what there was to know. Only a few of the game's pieces were still missing, the largest of them the one that had eluded him from the first — the significance of Fowler Alley.

18
SABINA

Madame Louella's fortune-telling parlor was one of several such establishments on the section of Kearney Street north of Market. There were a number of fortune-tellers doing business here, as well as such other charlatans as hypnotists, clairvoyants, astral seers, astrologists, phrenologists, even an alectromancer with cages full of roosters — all operating cheek by jowl with saloons, painless dentists, postcard sellers (which no doubt included the French variety sold from under the counter), auction houses, cheap clothing stores, and shooting galleries. During the evening hours the area was packed with crowds of citizens taking part in the nightly ritual stroll along what was known as the Cocktail Route, from the Reception Saloon on Sutter to the Palace Hotel Bar at Third and Market and scores of watering holes in between. Here, flaring torches and Salvation Army band music and the cries of sellers and pitchmen created a carnival-like atmosphere that would last for several hours.

This evening's bacchanal was in full swing when Sabina arrived shortly before seven o'clock. She had walked the "Ambrosial Path" before, most recently on the trail of a vicious woman pickpocket at the beginning of what she and John termed the Bughouse Affair — one of the few women to do so who was not trolling *nymphes du pavé*. As a result she moved swiftly through the crush of humanity here, ignoring the entreaties of the hawkers and the bold stares and bolder comments of well-dressed men and street characters alike, many of whom were deep in drink.

Her destination, a narrow storefront on the block between Bush and Pine, was flanked on one side by a charlatan who billed himself as "The Napoleon of Necromancers" and on the other by MRS. BRADLEY, FASHIONABLE CLOAK MAKING. A large sign above the entrance proclaimed:

MADAME LOUELLA
FUTURES TOLD — 25¢
SEES ALL, KNOWS ALL, TELLS ALL!

Sabina detoured around a lady of the

evening touting her charms to a well-dressed businessman and climbed a short flight of stairs to the second floor. The fortune-teller's door was covered with symbols — stars, planets, fog formations — that Madame Louella claimed were native to the Gypsy tribes of Transylvania where she'd been born. This was a patent fabrication. Sabina knew for a fact that the woman had been born Louella Green in Ashtabula, Ohio, where she'd been a problem child — truancy, shoplifting. When a band of confidence tricksters temporarily posing as patent medicine drummers had passed through on their way west, she had persuaded them to take her along. It was from them she'd learned the Gypsy fortune-telling dodge.

A bell above the door tinkled as Sabina entered the narrow anteroom with its three wooden chairs, all of which were empty. The odor of incense, meant to be exotic but in fact decidedly unpleasant, dilated her nostrils. The black curtain, decorated with more "magic" symbols, that separated the anteroom from the inner chamber parted almost immediately and Madame Louella's turbaned head poked out. Her professional smile changed shape when she saw Sabina.

"Ah, good," she said in her deep, almost

masculine voice, "you received my message. Come in, dearie, come in. No one else is here. Let me just lock the door to insure our privacy."

The rest of the woman's large body appeared, draped as usual in her flowing robe of a somewhat tarnished gold color, emblazoned with a different set of cabalistic signs in black and crimson. The turban was gold as well, with a large blue jewel, obviously a cheap paste imitation, set into the middle of it like a third eye. Strands of none too clean curly black hair straggled from beneath the cloth.

She produced a key from somewhere inside her robe. "Not that this is necessary," she said mournfully as she locked the door. "Business has been dreadful lately, I might even say nonexistent. Not a fortune to be told in three days, and only two the entire week. It's an affront to a woman born with Romany blood in her veins and the gift of peering through the mists of time to what lies ahead —"

"Your spiel is wasted on me, Louella, you should know that by now."

"Have you no sympathy, dearie? The fortune-telling racket really has been poor of late."

"A sign of the times."

"Yes, and not likely to change in the forseeable future."

Madame Louella cackled at her little joke, one Sabina had heard before, then resumed her mournful pose as she led the way through the black curtain into her "fortune room." The enclosure was small and dark, the walls painted black and unadorned, the single window thickly curtained to keep out light and mute the sounds of Cocktail Route revelry on the street below. It contained nothing other than a table draped in black cloth and two facing chairs. On the table sat one of the largest crystal globes Sabina had ever seen, treated with some sort of phosphorescent chemical that made it appear to emit an eerie inner glow, the room's only illumination.

The fortune-teller's chair was large and pillowed; Madame Louella sighed again as she lowered herself into it. "How much will my finder's fee be?" she asked when Sabina was seated across from her.

"That depends on exactly what you have to tell me."

"Ten dollars' worth, I should say."

"We'll see."

"I'm in arrears on my rent, dearie. Living hand to mouth."

Sabina doubted that. Madame Louella

may or may not have few customers wanting their futures told, but as part of the thriving network of information sellers she made enough to keep her rent current and her larder reasonably full.

"Business first. Your message said you'd know the whereabouts of Artemas Sneed by seven o'clock."

"And so I do. One of my friends" — Madame Louella's word for her coterie of informants — "brought the information shortly before you arrived. I had to pay him five dollars for his efforts."

Sabina doubted that, too, but she made no comment.

"I shouldn't tell you how he came by it, but I will," Madame Louella said in an obvious effort to curry largesse. "He shared a cell with Artemas Sneed for two years in San Quentin, and by chance encountered him a few nights ago in a Barbary Coast deadfall. It took him most of the day to find out where Sneed is living."

"And that is?"

"A rooming house on the waterfront. The name and address are surely worth ten dollars."

"If in fact the information is correct."

"It is. My friend guarantees it."

"Secondhand guarantees are not always

reliable," Sabina said. "I'll let you have five dollars now and five more after Sneed's lodgings have been confirmed."

"Oh, now, dearie . . ."

"I've always been fair with you, haven't I?"

"Yes, but given my financial difficulties, it's a hard bargain you drive."

"Hard times, hard bargains."

Madame Louella heaved another of her sighs. This was an old game between them, a form of haggling that the fortune-teller seemed to enjoy indulging in. Sabina didn't, but patience and a firm stance eventually brought the desired results.

"Very well, then, Mrs. Carpenter. But I'll have the first five dollars in advance, if you please."

"Done."

Sabina produced a five-dollar gold piece from her bag and Madame Louella made it disappear as quickly as if she were performing a conjurer's trick. Her thin mouth stretched in a satisfied smile; in the glow from the crystal globe, her eyes had an unnatural brightness in her round, pale face. Not for the first time in these surroundings, Sabina was reminded of nothing so much as the witch in "Hansel and Gretel."

"The Wanderer's Rest," Madame Louella

said. "Number one-twenty Davis Street, room three."

"Using his real name?"

"Yes."

"How long has he resided there?"

"Not long, according to my friend. Less than two weeks."

"And how long has he been out of prison?"

"About the same length of time. Paroled for good behavior." Madame Louella cackled, a sound that made her seem even more witchlike.

"What is he doing for money?"

"He told my friend he had irons in the fire."

"Irons in the fire, that's all?"

"Wouldn't admit to anything else."

"In which deadfall did your friend encounter him?"

"He didn't say. I'll ask him . . . for another two dollars."

"Greed is the devil's handmaiden, Louella."

"Phooey. Shall I ask him?"

"Only if it becomes necessary."

Sabina got to her feet. Madame Louella remained seated, peering up at her. "Will you bring the other five dollars tonight?"

"If I can. More likely it will be tomorrow."

"Are you heading off to find Sneed now? Yes? Well, be careful, dearie. Very careful in that neighborhood at night. I wouldn't want anything to happen to you."

"Or your five dollars."

"Ah, you know me so well. Or my five dollars."

The driver of the hack Sabina hailed on Market Street was dubious about her destination. "Are you sure that's where you want to go, lady? Davis Street's a fair rough place after dark."

"I'm sure. I may or may not be there long. Will you agree to wait for me?"

It was plain that he disliked the idea, but the offer of double the amount of the fare convinced him and brought his reluctant promise. She sat back as he cracked his whip and set them in motion, her bag with the derringer's comforting weight on her lap.

Both the cabbie and Madame Louella were right about the neighborhood, though it was not as rough as it had once been. Part of the section of the northern waterfront stretching from Pacific Avenue to Filbert Street, it contained warehouses and lodging places that had once catered exclusively to sailors off, or awaiting service on, the multitude of ships anchored in the Bay. During the Gold Rush era and for many years afterward, John had once told her, the area had been second only to the Barbary Coast as a hotbed of shanghaiing; crimps and boardinghouse masters had worked hand in hand to drug, rob, and consign hundreds of sailors to venal ship captains who then forced them to labor at sea under harsh conditions for no pay. One of the most notorious of the shanghaiers, an evil old woman named Miss Piggott, had operated a saloon and lodging house on Davis Street, Sabina remembered. Nowadays, with the practice of shanghaiing on the wane owing in part to the activities of the Sailors' Union of the Pacific, the rooming houses in the district were no longer such treacherous places, though they accommodated riffraff such as Artemas Sneed as well as able-bodied seamen.

John would have had a howling fit if he knew she was on her way to Davis Street, alone after dark, in the hope of confronting a likely dangerous ex-convict. A fool's errand, he would have called it. Stephen would have agreed; he had often chastised her for being fearless to the point of recklessness at times. Well, perhaps this was something of a reckless undertaking, but she was determined to get to the bottom of the business with Carson and Artemas Sneed as quickly as possible.

John's protectiveness toward her was not the same as her dear late husband's, of course. Or was it? Neither underestimated her ability to take care of herself, or possessed the old-fashioned chivalrous notion that women should at all times be kept out of harm's way; and John, too, genuinely cared for her. Once she'd believed his feelings were motivated by seduction alone, but she was no longer convinced of it. It was entirely possible that he fancied himself in love with her, that he yearned to occupy the empty space in her heart Stephen's death had created — a prospect which made her uncomfortable in the extreme. . . .

She forced her mind free of such speculation as the hansom rattled onto the Embarcadero and north past the Ferry House. John and their complicated relationship seemed to be creeping into her thoughts more and more of late, but this was hardly the time to be worrying about such matters.

Another ten minutes had passed when the driver made the turn onto Davis Street. This was the first Sabina had seen of the area at night and it did indeed appear mean and dreary. It was lighted by street lamps, some with broken globes, but so palely that the shadows beyond their reach were thick and black as ebony. The long bulky shape of a warehouse loomed along one side; on the other stood rows of two- and three-story board-and-batten structures, all lodging houses except for a saloon on the corner of the next block — rat-infested firetraps dating back to the Gold Rush era. Lamplight glowed behind a few windows, diffused and dulled by grime- and salt-caked glass. The street was deserted, only a scattered few pedestrians abroad on the boardwalks.

The Wanderer's Rest turned out to be the third rooming house beyond the saloon. When the driver drew up in front, he stayed on the box; not for him the gentlemanly act of helping a lady passenger alight in this neighborhood. He leaned down as Sabina stepped out into a shivery wind off the Bay, nervously asked for half the agreed-upon fare. She refused; if she paid him the half, he might not wait for her.

She turned away from his protest, drawing her cape tightly around her shoulders, and hurried along a cracked brick path leading to the Wanderer's Rest. The faint, tinny sound of a badly played piano came from the corner saloon; a pair of angry voices rose briefly inside the lodging house next door. Otherwise the night was quiet. A scrawny cat darted across in front of her and disappeared into the shadows as she mounted rickety steps to the entrance.

The door, fortunately, was unlatched. Sabina stepped into a gloomy, gaslit vestibule heavy with damp, stale air; two closed doors faced each other on either side of a staircase leading to the upper floors. Sneed's room, number 3, would be on the second floor. She lifted her skirts and made the climb slowly to minimize the creak of warped stair risers.

The hallway was so poorly lit that she had to peer closely at the first door she encountered to make out a crudely painted numeral 3. A thin strip of lamplight shone at the bottom of the door, indicating that the room was occupied. She slid her hand inside her bag, grasped the derringer's handle, then laid her ear close to the door to listen. No sounds came from within. She drew the Remington and tapped its short barrel on the panel.

The door was off its latch; she heard a faint creak and another thin strip of light appeared along its vertical edge. There was no response to the knock, nor to a second. Sabina held a deep breath, raised the derringer, and pushed the door inward with her free hand.

What she saw brought a sharp release of the held breath. Yes, the room was occupied, but not in the way she'd expected. The man lying curled on his side on the bare floor, a patch of blood gleaming on the front of his linsey-woolsey shirt and eyes open wide in a sightless stare, was quite plainly dead.

19
SABINA

Sabina stepped quickly inside, easing the door shut behind her. This was not the first time she'd encountered a victim of lethal violence, but the suddenness of her discovery and the stench of death that permeated the sparsely furnished room caused her gorge to rise. She locked her throat muscles and took several deep breaths to steady herself before she approached the body.

She had never seen the man before. He had been in his forties, partially bald, his craggy face pale-skinned beneath a thin growth of reddish whiskers. Roughly dressed, although the boots he wore looked to be new and fairly expensive. Artemas Sneed? The pale skin prison pallor?

She bent to gingerly place two fingers against a none too clean neck. The flesh was pliant, still warm. Not long dead, she judged, no more than two hours, perhaps as little as one.

A pistol was loosely gripped in his right hand, but the absence of a gunpowder smell told Sabina that it hadn't been fired. And that he hadn't been shot. She peered more closely at the chest wound, and saw then with some surprise that there was a similar wound in his back. Slits, both of them, thin and half an inch in width. Neither had bled much; death must have been instantaneous. No knife of any sort had made those slits, but rather something long and thin that had been thrust into him with enough force to pass all the way through his body. Not so much stabbed as skewered.

By what type of weapon? A saber, possibly, but hardly anyone carried one in San Francisco, not even the officers stationed at the Presidio. A sword cane, more likely. Many men carried such instruments, respectable citizens for self-protection (John had one that had served him on more than one occasion), the more sophisticated breed of criminal for intimidation and assault.

There was no sign of the weapon in any case; the murderer had wiped it off on the linsey-woolsey shirt — bloody smears on one shoulder attested to that — and taken it away with him. An overturned chair and a cot askew against one wall indicated a brief struggle before the fatal blow was struck. Some sort of confrontation, perhaps over money? Possibly, but not between Sneed and another man of his ilk. Pistols and knives and coshes were their weapons of choice.

Sabina steeled herself, breathing through her mouth, and knelt to search the man's clothing. In one trouser pocket she found a purse, inside of which was a small wad of greenbacks and two five-dollar gold pieces — a total of more than sixty dollars. Robbery hadn't figured in the killing, then. Which likely meant that the murderer was someone other than a Barbary Coast felon.

There was nothing on the body to identify the dead man. A small wardrobe contained an inexpensive sack coat, a pair of trousers, and two shirts; the pockets in all were empty. A cloth travel bag under the cot yielded nothing, either, and the only items on a low table beside the cot were a packet of matches and another of cheroots.

Was the victim Artemas Sneed? It seemed probable, since this was his room. If so, a man with Sneed's background and propensities might have more than a few enemies. Any one of them might have ended his life, for any of a hundred reasons. He was also an alleged blackmailer, and blackmailers often preyed on more than one victim.

Blackmail could have been the source of the sixty dollars he carried. But then so could gambling, and such crimes as petty theft, armed robbery, and fraud.

And then there was the type of weapon that had been used. . . .

Carson? Oh, Lord, could Carson have done this?

The thought opened a hollow feeling inside Sabina. He didn't seem the type of man capable of killing another in such a brutal fashion as this, even in self-defense, but then neither did he seem the type to have been involved in a gold-stealing scheme that left him open to extortion. She simply didn't know him well enough to make an accurate judgment. One thing she did know: The type of long, slender stick he carried *could* conceal a deadly piece of steel.

The time had come to face him with her suspicions; she couldn't put it off any longer. Whether he was innocent or guilty of any magnitude of wrongdoing, she would be able to tell it from his responses and his demeanor. No man had ever successfully lied to her about an important issue such as this. She fervently hoped Carson would not try.

The Nob Hill mansion owned by Carson's

father occupied most of a steep block of California Street not far from Huntington Park, on the opposite slope from the Blanchford estate. It was similar in style to the grand French Second Empire–style home built by Leland Stanford, one of the "Big Four" tycoons and architect of the Union Pacific Railroad, though smaller and not quite as elaborately designed. Even at night, illuminated by street lamps and a scattering of electric lights, the three-story, mansard-roofed edifice and its surrounding gardens were impressive.

After alighting from the hansom, Sabina once again asked the driver to wait for her. The cab fare was already substantial; a few dollars more wouldn't and didn't matter. The driver was as happy to bring her here as he had been to depart Davis Street and its dismal environs. The fact that his passenger had chosen to travel from squalor to the height of wealth obviously puzzled him, but to his credit he held his tongue.

Sabina hurried through a gate in the spike-tipped iron fence that enclosed the Montgomery property, then through a considerable amount of greenery to the house. A heavy bronze lion's head knocker made a booming noise when she lifted it and let it fall. The door was opened after a short wait by a middle-aged butler in full dress livery. If he was surprised to see a comely young woman calling alone at this late hour, he didn't show it.

"Yes, madam?"

"I'm an acquaintance of Mr. Carson Montgomery," she said, and presented her card along with her name. "I'd like to speak to him if he's home."

"I'm afraid he isn't."

Damn! "Gone out for the evening at what time?"

"To my knowledge, he has been away since early this morning."

"I see. Do you know where I might find him?"

"I do not. Nor when he might return."

"Then I'll leave a message for him."

"As you wish."

"A *written* message." Frustration sharpened Sabina's voice. "In a sealed envelope."

The butler was unperturbed. "Certainly, madam. Would you like me to supply stationery and a pen?"

"A sheet of paper and an envelope, yes. I have a pen."

"Very good." He studied her for a moment, apparently decided she was respectable and not likely to steal anything if left alone, and said as if bestowing a favor, "You may enter and wait in the drawing room."

The high-ceilinged drawing room was empty except for heavy Victorian furnishings and several large paintings of members of the Montgomery clan, most of them done at advanced ages and rather forbiddingly austere. Sabina fancied the multitude of eyes appraising her as she stood waiting. None of the chairs and settees looked the least bit comfortable.

When the butler returned, she took to a secretary desk the letter-sized sheet of vellum and matching envelope he handed her. Both pieces of stationery bore an embossed Montgomery family crest. She wrote Carson's name on the envelope, checked the time on the grandfather clock across the room, and then proceeded to write her message.

Thursday, 9:20 P.M.

Carson:
I must speak with you on a matter of considerable urgency. Will you be so good as to meet me tomorrow at one P.M. in the Grand Central Court at the Palace Hotel? If you are unable to do so, please let me know at my office by telephone or messenger, but I sincerely

hope that will not be necessary.

Sabina

She folded the paper and sealed it into the envelope, which she then gave to the butler. "Please put this where Carson will be certain to see it when he comes home."

"Very well, madam." He held the envelope gingerly between thumb and forefinger as he ushered her out, as if he couldn't wait to be rid of it.

Sabina gave the waiting hack driver her home address and settled back on the cushions. She felt almost relieved that Carson had not been at home tonight. Coming here had been an impetuous act; it would have been awkward and unpleasant confronting him, implying criminal guilt if not actually accusing him of it, in his own home. A public place such as the Palace Hotel was more suitable for the task.

She wondered if she should have requested an earlier meeting time in her message. This distressing situation with Carson and the Gold King scandal and the death of Artemas Sneed was a heavy weight on her mind; the sooner she had a firm grasp on the truth, the better able she'd be to deal with it. But no, one o'clock was soon enough. She might well have pressing agency business to attend to in the morning.

Briefly she considered, as she had on the ride up from Davis Street, whether she should notify the police — anonymously — of the dead man in Sneed's room at the Wanderer's Rest. It was the proper thing to do. John might be cavalier about bending and breaking the law, but she wasn't; Stephen and the other Pinkerton agents she'd known had taught her to obey it except in incidents of dire necessity. There was no such necessity in this case. The body would be discovered soon enough, she had no specific knowledge of who had committed the crime, and the police would have little interest in the violent death of an ex-convict and Barbary Coast hanger-on — except, she thought wryly, to "confiscate as evidence" the sixty dollars in his purse if the money was still there when they arrived on the scene. Only the hack driver had seen her entering and leaving the rooming house, she was sure of that, and he would have no reason to come forward; homicides were so common in the rougher sections of the city that they were seldom reported in the newspapers. Her wisest course of action was to do nothing at all until she met with Carson tomorrow.

She closed her eyes, shifted her tired body

into a more comfortable position, and let the rattling of the wheels and clopping of the horse's hooves lull her into a half-doze the rest of the journey to Russian Hill.

20
QUINCANNON

Friday morning was bright, sunny, the air crisp and winey as well as briny, and Quincannon whistled "The Drunkard's Funeral," one of his collection of temperance tunes, as he alighted from the Powell Street cable car and proceeded at a brisk pace down Market Streeet. The briefcase he carried swung loosely at his side, but his grip on it could not have been tighter.

For once, he arrived at the office before Sabina. The morning mail had already been delivered; he scooped it up from the floor under the mail slot and tossed it on his desk. Went to turn up the steam heat to dispel the lingering night's chill, then knelt and twirled the combination lock to open the office safe. It was a Mosler, one of the best manufacturers of strongboxes; large, bolted to the floor, and as secure as any private business could expect. Far more secure than the small one in his bedroom.

He opened the briefcase and transferred the files he'd appropriated from James Scarlett's law office to the safe. They constituted important evidence and now he didn't have to worry about their safety until the time came to turn them over to the authorities.

The mail wasn't such-a-much — only one containing a check in payment for services rendered, the rest circulars, bills, this month's issue of the *Police Gazette.* There was also a sealed envelope with "Mrs. Carpenter" scrawled on it in a barely legible backhand. The writing was familiar, that of the news vendor, Slewfoot, one of their more reliable informants. A communication from him, as from others in the city-wide network of information sellers, was often delivered in this fashion after office hours.

He was putting the envelope and the bills on Sabina's desk blotter when the telephone bell jangled. Alexander Graham Bell's invention had its uses, but he had yet to get used to the sudden shrill clamor of its summons. He cut off the noise on its second ring.

A woman's imperious voice said, "Is that you, Blackbeard?"

Mrs. Harriet Blanchford. Not even such as the Blackbeard slight bothered him this morning. He said cheerfully, "John Quincannon, Mrs. Blanchford," listened, said, "No, Mrs. Carpenter, hasn't come in yet this morning. I imagine she'll arrive shortly." Listened some more and then said, "Yes, I'll make sure she gets the message," and was rewarded with an abrupt termination of the call. Ah, well, the elderly had their privileges, a tolerable amount of rude behavior among them. The more so when the party involved was wealthy and destined to be another satisfied client.

He would be leaving shortly, so he sat down to commit Harriet Blanchford's message to paper. He was in the process when the door opened to admit his erstwhile and much coveted partner.

"Good morning, my dear. Beautiful day, isn't it."

"Is it?" she said. Her tone was uncharacteristically bleak. "What makes you so jolly today?"

"Considerable progress on the Scarlett case. What makes you so dispirited?"

Sabina didn't respond. Instead, she went about unpinning her hat and hanging up her cape on the coat tree. He inspected her more closely as she did so, and what he saw was alarming. She looked even more tired today, her eyes betokening a sleep-deprived night. There was a remoteness about them, too, as if her mind were heavily burdened. And her mouth and jaw bore the kind of tightness that came from teeth-clenching. Carson Montgomery again? If the man had harmed or severely upset her in any way . . .

Quincannon watched her sit at her desk. She noticed the "Mrs. Carpenter" envelope immediately, opened it, read the paper inside without a change of expression, reinserted it, and put it aside.

"Good news?" he asked.

"Expected news."

"The Blanchford case?"

"Yes. Is this the only message that came for me?"

"Were you hoping for another?"

"No. Just the opposite."

"Well, I have more Blanchford news for you," he said. "The widow telephoned not five minutes ago. It seems the kidnappers kept their promise after all."

"Her husband's body is back in the family crypt?"

"Brought there and deposited sometime last night. Her son found it there this morning." Sabina's expression prompted him to add, "You don't seem surprised."

"I'm not. Also as I expected."

"The body was returned in the same

251

mysterious manner as its taking, Mrs. Blanchford said. What did she mean by that?"

"It was allegedly stolen in what appeared to be an impossible fashion, the crypt being still sealed with no tampering of its door lock and Mrs. Blanchford in possession of the only key."

This announcement warped Quincannon's brow. He said, "And returned in the same fashion, evidently, if the crypt was locked again this morning."

"Not quite, but close enough."

"So. A seemingly impossible crime, and you didn't tell me about it?"

"I didn't need to."

"You mean you've solved the mystery? How?"

"That's a silly question, John. By detective work and deductive reasoning, of course. You don't honestly believe you're the only one adept at that sort of conundrum, do you?"

"No, but I've had a great deal of experience —"

"And I haven't? Oh, but naturally my skills are nowhere as preeminent as yours."

Quincannon felt himself being boxed into an uncomfortable corner. He squirmed his way to safety by saying, "That's not true.

They're every bit the match of mine," but the words weren't merely a convenient sop; he meant them, much as it bruised his ego to admit it. "So now you know who's behind the Blanchford snatch."

Sabina seemed mollified, at least temporarily. "Who, and how their tricks were worked. A bumbling fool's game from start to finish."

"How so?"

Instead of answering his question, she changed the subject — or so he thought at first — by asking a question of her own. "Have you found out the significance of Fowler Alley yet?"

"Fowler Alley? No, but I will."

"Yes. Right now."

"What do you mean?"

"I believe I know what it is."

"You do?" He peered at her with his head tipped forward like a crane's. "What? How?"

"You'll know when I tell you the solution to the Blanchford crime. The details make it apparent."

Sabina proceeded to do so, not taking time to savor her prowess as he might have done in a reversed role; her explanation was specifically brief and to the point. When she revealed the gaffe, he saw immediately how it related to James Scarlett's last words. He smote himself on the forehead. "By Jove, that must be the answer! I'm a rattlepate for not seeing it myself."

"Well, those are your words, not mine."

Quincannon bounced to his feet, favored her with a radiant smile as he clamped on his derby. "Sabina, my dear, you're truly wonderful. I could kiss you."

"If you try, I'll box your ears until they bleed."

He laughed, impudently blew her a kiss anyway from a safe distance, and then went haring out the door.

21
SABINA

It was a few minutes before noon when Sabina arrived at the Blanchfords' Nob Hill mansion. On the one hand she didn't relish her mission; on the other hand she was looking forward to it. Like John, she derived satisfaction from the successful conclusion to an investigation, even one as unpleasant as this. She could only hope that the matter with Carson could be untangled satisfactorily as well, for his sake as well as hers.

The houseman, Edmund, a thin old man with the face of a mournful hound, admitted her, left her waiting in the front hall while he went to announce her, and then showed her out to the side terrace where Harriet and Bertram Blanchford were having a late breakfast or early lunch at a table overlooking the rose garden. Mrs. Blanchford no longer seemed quite so frail today; her relief was evident in the erect set of her body, the color in her cheeks, the brightness of her eyes. She offered Sabina a thin but welcoming smile.

"I take it you're here because Blackbeard delivered my message?"

"Yes, as soon as I arrived at the office."

"I didn't expect you to come in person, but I'm not displeased that you did. Isn't the news splendid?"

Indeed it was, Sabina agreed, managing to keep tartness out of her voice. She declined a cup of tea, but accepted the widow's invitation to occupy the heavy wrought-iron chair between her and her son. Bertram was smoking an expensive cigar — evidently Mrs. Blanchford's prejudice against tobacco didn't extend to the outdoors — and wearing an expression of smug solemnity.

"Paying the ransom demand was absolutely the right thing to do, Mrs. Carpenter," he said. "When I opened the mausoleum this morning, there Father was — back safe and sound in his casket. Though how he was returned is as much a mystery as how he was taken. The door was locked as before and nothing was disturbed."

"So I understand." Sabina shifted her gaze to his mother. "I'd like another look at the crypt, if you don't mind."

"Why do you find it necessary?"

"I have my reasons."

"Very well, then."

"Will you accompany me, Mr. Blanch-ford?"

Bertram shrugged. "As you wish."

Mrs. Blanchford took the large brass key from her dress pocket, handed it to him. As before he fetched a lantern from inside the house, then he and Sabina set off to where the mausoleum squatted, cool and dark, at the foot of the garden. When the heavy bronze door was unlocked, the young man stepped back and to one side.

"I'll wait here while you have your look inside."

"I have no need for a look inside."

"But you said —"

"A ruse to bring you down here alone." Sabina fixed him with a narrowed and knowing eye. "Now, then. Where is the ransom money?"

"What?"

"Have you shared it with your confederate and debtors yet? Or is it all still in your possession?"

"I . . . I have no idea what you're talking about."

"Oh, yes you do. You no more delivered the seventy-five thousand dollars to Golden Gate Park than I flew upside down in the last windstorm. The plain truth is, you're the one who planned this body-snatching business. And wrote and 'delivered' the ransom demands."

Bertram blinked, sputtered, then made an effort to draw himself up indignantly. "That's a slanderous accusation. How dare you!"

"A copycat crime if ever there was one. Inspired by the newspaper accounts of the Chinese tong leader's stolen remains that appeared just after your father's death. There's no use denying it."

"I do deny it. You know full well that I had no access to the key, no way of getting inside the crypt —"

"Nonsense," Sabina said. "All that mystification was designed to cloud the truth, keep your mother from becoming suspicious, and focus attention on a nonexistent gang of body snatchers. There is no mystery about the alleged disappearance of your father's body or its delivery last night."

Bertram wagged his head, but not in denial. His eyes had already taken on the shine of a trapped animal's.

"We both know the body was never in the mausoleum," Sabina said. "It was removed from the casket at the Evergreen Chapel, after the service and before the procession here. The casket is heavy and your father was a slight man — you counted on none of the pallbearers noticing the disparity in weight and none did. Joshua Trilby did the removal work, under the guise of a faked delay with the hearse. He also cut the piece from the satin lining and removed the ring, which he then turned over to you, and stored the body at the mortuary until last night.

"Its reappearance was even more simply managed. The mausoleum key was still in your mother's possession, though not as well cared for because of the circumstances. I expect you managed to appropriate it while she was asleep. You came down here to meet Trilby at a prearranged time, opened the crypt, helped him with the transfer, locked the door again afterward, and put the key back where you got it. Then, this morning, you pretended to discover your father's shell."

"How . . . how could you know . . ."

"I began to suspect the truth when I examined the empty casket," Sabina said. "If a gang of genuine body snatchers had been at work, all the heavy silver handles and other valuable silver trim would have been stolen as well. The casket's pillow bed was just as telltale. If a body had lain there for even a short length of time, the satin would have retained some impression of it. But there was none; it was completely smooth."

Bertram said desperately, "If Trilby is guilty, he acted alone. I'm a wealthy man, I have no need for a large sum of cash. . . ."

"You're *not* a wealthy man. The estate your father left is not nearly as large as has been generally assumed, and as you no doubt knew; the Blanchford Investment Foundation drained away much of your father's wealth, and ill-advised stock-market purchases depleted it further." This information had come from the financial wizard Matthew Wainwright. What she went on to say was courtesy of Slewfoot. "Your own funds you depleted with large bets on slow horses and your impulsive investment in the Ingleside racetrack. You're presently in debt to Billy the Bookie and other sure-thing operators, and you have no means of borrowing enough to pay the markers. Your mother controls the family purse strings and she doesn't approve of your passion for horse racing and your penchant for consorting with touts and bookmakers. Don't bother to deny any of that, either. I know it all for a fact."

Bertram's mouth hinged open, clamped

shut again. His face had paled to the color of tallow.

"Trilby also has financial troubles, partly the result of mismanagement of his mortuary and partly horse-race gambling losses. Birds of a feather. You met him at one of the county fair races — you were seen together at the Alameda and other tracks on several occasions, thick as the thieves you are. You had no trouble talking him into becoming your accomplice in the scheme to dupe your mother, I'm sure."

A sound halfway between a moan and a goat's bleat escaped Bertram's throat. He took a half-step toward Sabina. For an instant she thought he might attempt to attack her. Even though she knew him to be a weakling and likely a coward, she had been prepared for any rash act on his part; throughout the confrontation she'd kept her hand inside her bag, her fingers clutching the handle of the Remington derringer. But Bertram's half-step was merely reflexive. There was no fight in the man; she would have no trouble with him.

There was no bluster left in him, either. "I had to do it," he said, abandoning all pretense of innocence. "I *had* to. Threats of bodily harm if I didn't pay my markers . . . I had to do something!"

"The ransom money. Do you still have it?"

"Yes, in my office downtown. I intended to pay Trilby and the bookmakers tonight, but now —"

"Now you'll make an excuse to your mother and together we'll go fetch it. I'll see that it's returned to her."

"And tell her that I — No, you can't do that! She'll be devastated, she'll disown me!"

"You should have thought of that," Sabina said, "before you decided to become a ghoul."

22

QUINCANNON

The day had turned overcast, the temperature several degrees colder, when Quincannon turned afoot into Fowler Alley. A sharp wind gusted along its nearly empty expanse, swirling refuse and grit from the pitted roadway. All of Chinatown had a desolate aspect today, like a place where most of the inhabitants have fled to avoid a plague. Very few Chinese were abroad; there seemed to be almost as many uniformed policemen walking the streets singly and in pairs, keeping the peace.

Quincannon made his way slowly along the first block, hands buried in the pockets of his Chesterfield, his shoulders hunched and his roving gaze studying the buildings with their grimy windows and indecipherable calligraphy. All seemed too small and closely packed to be the one he sought. He entered the second block. Halfway along he spied the one he should have noticed on his previous visit, one that was larger than the rest with an alleyway along one side that appeared wide enough to accommodate a carriage.

He crossed the cobbled street, stepped into the deserted alley. As he moved deeper into its gloomy expanse, he saw that it was a cul-de-sac that widened at its end, where an intersecting passage ran along the rear of the building. He hurried to the corner, poked his head around. Ah, yes! Parked in the shadows some twenty yards distant was a high-sided black wagon, unhitched and unattended, waiting.

Quincannon made his way to the rig along heavily rutted ground. One quick look up close was enough to confirm its purpose and that this was the place he'd come looking for.

The wagon was the Chinese version of a hearse, the building an undertaking parlor.

Just beyond the rig's backside, a closed door was set into the wall — the parlor's rear entrance. A tight little smile split Quincannon's beard when he found the door neither barred nor latched. He eased it open with his left hand, sliding the Navy Colt from its holster with his right. The pale glow from a pair of hanging lanterns showed him a storage area and a corridor that led

264

from it toward the front, both empty. From somewhere in that direction the singsong voices of two or three Chinese came to him, but back here there was only silence.

His eyes had grown accustomed to the gloom; he had no difficulty making his way across the room, the warped floorboards creaking from his weight but not loudly enough for the sounds to carry. He stepped into the corridor, tiptoeing. Halfway along, the sickish odor of formaldehyde dilated his nostrils, forcing him to breathe through his mouth.

The chamber into which he emerged, likewise lantern lit and empty, contained several coffins, most of them unadorned pine boxes designed for the lowborn, a few of the lacquered teakwood variety favored by the highborn and wealthy. A tapestry-covered doorway opened to the right. He moved ahead to the doorway, brushed the fabric aside.

Here was the embalming room, the source of the formaldehyde odor. He traversed the room past a metal table, an herb cabinet, a second cabinet in which needles, razors, and other tools of the mortician's trade gleamed behind glass. The doorway at the far side was covered by a regular wooden door instead of a tapestry; when he opened it and stepped through, he found himself in a small enclosure so ice-chilled that his expelled breath showed vaporously. The little room contained nothing more than three slender storage vaults.

Sabina had been right, by Godfrey. He was sure of it even before he began opening the vaults.

The first was empty. The second was occupied by the husk of a very old Mandarin whose skin was so wrinkled he might have been mummified. The third was the right one.

The embalmed body here was also that of an old man, but one who had lived a much more pampered life. It was dressed in an intricately embroidered robe of gold silk; the cheeks had been powdered, the long queue neatly braided, and the thin drooping mustache trimmed. A parchment-paged prayerbook was still clutched between gnarled hands.

"Bing Ah Kee," Quincannon said under his breath, "or I'll eat my hat and Mock Quan's for dessert."

He slid the vault closed, retraced his steps to the doorway, swept the door open. And came face-to-face with a youngish Chinese wearing a stained leather apron over his blouse and pantaloons.

The youth let out a startled bleat, followed by an exclamation or epithet that threatened to escalate into a full-fledged cry of alarm. As he turned to flee, his voice just starting to rise, Quincannon fetched him a sharp rap with the barrel of the Navy at the spot where pigtail met scalp. Flight and cry both ended immediately.

Quincannon hopped over the fallen man, abandoning stealth in his run across the coffin room into the rear corridor, then across the storage area to the rear door. Behind him he could hear raised voices and the sounds of pursuit. He flung the door open, ducked into the alleyway. Squeezed past the hearse and raced to the side passage.

He was two steps into that narrow way when the bullet came within inches of puncturing a vital portion of his anatomy.

The crack of the pistol and its muzzle flash gave him a glimpse of the shooter's location — close to the funeral parlor wall, just inside the passage from Fowler Alley — as he hurled himself sideways and down to the foul-smelling earth. He fetched up as a second bullet pierced the air above him, snap-fired an answering shot with his Navy. He'd had no time to aim, but his slug must have likewise come close to hitting its target — close enough to put an abrupt end to the ambush. The black-clad figure wheeled backward from the wall, disappeared around the corner into Fowler Alley.

Quincannon scrambled to his feet and launched into a stumbling pursuit. He emerged in time to see his quarry running diagonally across the narrow street some twenty rods distant, passing so close in front of an oncoming wagon that the horse reared in fright. The animal's flashing hooves narrowly missed him as it buck-jumped forward. The assassin staggered, nearly fell before he regained his balance. In that moment Quincannon, on the run and closing the gap, had a clear look at the man's face.

Mock Quan, in his highbinder's guise.

Recognition stoked Quincannon's wrath. Twice now that damned young hoodlum had tried to ventilate him, and by all the saints he was not going to have a third opportunity!

Mock Quan was no longer the coolly devious plotter; panic had him in its grip now. The fact that he'd made this assassination attempt in broad daylight — he must have been inside the parlor, gone back out the front way when the commotion started — was an indication of just how desperate he'd become. What scant few pedestrians there were scattered as he dashed up onto the sidewalk, his weapon, as was Quincannon's, still in hand. Startled voices rose, a woman shrieked as if imitating a fire siren.

The chase had covered nearly half a block when Mock Quan barged into a sidewalk fruit and vegetable cart, toppling it and sending oranges, apples, cabbages, and assorted other comestibles rolling and thumping into the street. Though the collision staggered him again, he managed to stay on his feet. He cast a look over his shoulder, saw that his pursuer's long-legged stride had halved the distance between them, and lurched sideways through a storefront doorway whose wind-whipped pennant identified it as a restaurant.

When Quincannon reached the eatery and flung himself inside, he immediately spied Mock Quan halfway across a long open dining area, just swinging around to face toward him. Mock Quan fired a wild shot, the lead pellet chipping wood from the wallboard two feet from the door as Quincannon dodged aside and dropped into a crouch. The handful of frightened patrons also threw themselves out of harm's way, upsetting tables, filling the air with bowls of food and flying chopsticks. Quincannon held his fire; an answering shot would have been foolishly risky. Mock Quan didn't fire again, either. Instead he spun and raced away into a narrow passage at the rear.

Quincannon zigzagged after him through wreckage and cowering diners. The passage led into a steamy kitchen peopled by more frightened Chinese, at the far end of which was a door through which the fugitive was just shouldering. The door debouched into another alley — an alley open at one end, closed at the other. Quincannon's mouth twisted into a feral grin when he saw that his quarry had turned in the wrong direction.

Mock Quan's step faltered when he realized he had boxed himself in. He cast a brief look over his shoulder. If he had halted, with the intention of triggering another round, Quincannon would have had no qualms about firing back in self-defense. As it was, the damned young scoundrel kept on running to the end of the alley, where a door was set into a two-story, pagoda-style building that formed the end of the cul-de-sac. As furious as Quincannon was, he had never yet shot a criminal from behind and never would, not even to wound. He charged ahead, drawing to within a dozen paces as Mock Quan yanked the door open and plunged through.

Quincannon followed, stepped cautiously

into a tiny vestibule. Footfalls thudded on an ill-lighted staircase, then there was a metallic banging noise from above. He pounded up to a second-floor landing, where to his right he came upon another set of stairs that evidently led up from Fowler Alley. To his left was a doorway with a wrought-iron gate that had been shoved wide open — the banging sound he'd heard from below. Beyond the gate was a small, shadow-ridden anteroom, a perfect place for another ambush.

But Mock Quan wasn't there; despite the blood-beat of exertion in his ears, Quincannon could make out the sounds of movement somewhere in a larger room that opened to his left, from which a reddish glow emanated. The bead curtain that separated the two spaces was still swaying and faintly clacking.

The noises stopped as he sidestepped to the curtain, carefully peered through. What he was looking at then was a temple, lit by several hanging red and gold lanterns. The pungent odor of incense came from a recessed side altar of red-painted wood with some sort of statue framed inside it. Lining one long sidewall were small altars, statues, teak tables, and other pieces of furniture, nearly all of them in red and gold. At the

271

far end stood a pair of large carved altars, one that took up the entire wall, the other, fronted by a red prayer bench, set apart in the middle of the floor.

There was no sign of Mock Quan. Trapped and hiding somewhere, no doubt preparing to make his final stand. Under one of the altars, all of which were draped in embroidered cloths? No. Arranged atop the cloths were bowls of fruit and flowers, joss urns, other items Quincannon couldn't identify, but he could see that none had been disturbed.

With his free hand he grasped several of the bead strands to keep them still as he eased through into the temple. Again to his left he spied a short ell that contained a red-painted platform supporting a drum and a heavy iron temple bell. This was where Mock Quan had gone. Quincannon sensed it even before the Chinese showed himself, coming up and out from behind the temple bell in such a violent hurry that he upset an ornamental altar standard, like a spear or pikestaff, and sent it clattering to the floor.

Mock Quan emitted a hissing noise loud enough to override the echoes created by the toppled standard, the pistol in his hand swinging up. Instinctively Quincannon ducked sideways, crouching again with his

Navy on a bead. But Mock Quan failed to fire, though not for lack of intent. His weapon was either empty or it had jammed.

He stood stock-still for two or three seconds, his finger futilely jerking at the trigger, the gun wobbling in his grasp. Quincannon could have put two or three rounds into him during those moments, but a felon captured alive was always preferable to a felon delivered dead, even one as scurrilous as Mock Quan. Besides which, the young scoundrel may have been willing to desecrate a temple with gunfire, but John Frederick Quincannon wasn't.

"Drop it and lift your hands, Mock Quan," he said. "You're done to a turn and you know it."

The Chinese didn't obey. He was still in the grip of his frenzy. He let out another shriek, hurled the weapon at Quincannon, and then charged him head down like a bull at a red cape.

Quincannon dodged the flying pistol, dodged the blind rush, and fetched the young rogue a solid blow on the temple with the Navy's barrel. Obligingly Mock Quan went down and out in a heap, the slouch hat coming off to reveal his disgraced red *mow-yung*.

Quincannon stood looking down at him.

He was no longer angry now that the chase and Mock Quan's vicious lust for power in Chinatown had both ended in a satisfactory fashion; just weary and contemplative. The difference between despots such as Little Pete and would-be despots such as Mock Quan, he mused, was that while both were rapacious and reckless, the true tyrant was too arrogant to give himself up to either desperation or panic. The would-be tyrant was far easier to bring down because his arrogance was no more than a thin membrane over the shell of cowardice.

It was Mock Quan, not Little Pete, who had proved to be the craven son of a turtle.

23

QUINCANNON

There was no way he was about to tax his already weary body by slinging Mock Quan over his shoulder and carrying him out of the temple building in search of police assistance. He settled for tearing the black tunic into strips and using them to bind the coward's hands and feet. Mock Quan was still unconscious when he finished.

It took him only a few short minutes to track down one of the police patrols. He identified himself and quickly explained the reasons for what had happened, including his discovery of Bing Ah Kee's remains. The patrolmen, fortunately, were among the brighter members of their breed; although skeptical at first, they agreed to a request that Lieutenant Price be notified immediately, and while one of them used a police call box to contact the Hall of Justice and request a paddy wagon, the other accompanied Quincannon to the temple.

Mock Quan was groggily awake by then, struggling in vain to free himself from his bonds. He attempted a bluff at first, claiming to the patrolman that the *fan kwei* detective had sought to murder him and he was the one who had acted in self-defense, but the words fell on deaf ears. Mock Quan's pistol — jammed, as it turned out — and his fear-raddled visage, coolie disguise, and highborn *mow yung* were sufficiently damning. When a pair of steel bracelets replaced the cloth strips binding his wrists, he lapsed into sullen silence.

Together, Quincannon and the copper hauled him downstairs to Fowler Alley, where they loaded him into the waiting paddy wagon. Quincannon readily agreed to go along. Not a word was spoken on the jouncing drive to the Hall of Justice; Mock Quan might have been a block of stone perched on the bench across from where Quincannon sat watching him with a basilisk eye.

Lieutenant Price and a glowering Sergeant Gentry were waiting at the booking desk when they arrived. The two officers listened to a brief account of the afternoon's events, after which Gentry said to Price, "Let me have him for five minutes alone, Lieutenant. I'll make him talk."

276

Quincannon said, "I would advise against that, Lieutenant."

Price agreed. "There'll be no more strong-arm tactics until we have this matter straightened out."

Mock Quan paid no attention to this exchange. He maintained his stoic silence throughout the booking process.

Quincannon drew Price aside, into the privacy of the muster room, where the ropes, firemen's axes, weapons, bulletproof vests, and other flying squad paraphernalia were still in evidence. Men had been dispatched to the undertaking parlor, the lieutenant said, to arrest anyone occupying the premises. And to claim Bing Ah Kee's husk, if it was still there, so it could be returned to its rightful place at the Four Families Temple.

"It will still be there," Quincannon said.

"What makes you so sure?"

"The mortician has nowhere to move the body on short notice, nor would he dare destroy it for fear of the wrath of the gods and all of Chinatown. Mock Quan was the motivating force behind it being stored there, either through threats or bribery."

"But how did you know that's where it was hidden?" Price asked. "And that it was Mock Quan who was behind the theft, and that he would be at the parlor this afternoon?"

"I didn't know he would be there," Quincannon said, "only having just deduced the significance of Fowler Alley." This was stretching the truth, but explaining Sabina's role would have required revealing confidential details of the Blanchford case. "Mock Quan's presence was a fortunate coincidence, as it turned out. He must have gone to the parlor to arrange for the body to be found in a place that would lay the blame for the snatch on Little Pete — lighting the final fuse to ignite full-scale tong warfare. And he wore his highbinder's disguise for the obvious reason of avoiding recognition on the streets by both his countrymen and the police patrols. As for the rest . . ."

"Yes?"

"It's a long story, Lieutenant. Would you mind if I told it to you in the company of Sergeant Gentry and Chief Crowley, if he's here?"

"He is. And as eager to hear your explanations as I am."

A short time later Quincannon and the three ranking officers were once again seated in the chief's private sanctum. Crowley's round, florid face had the same haggard appearance as Price's; Gentry, too, looked as if he had had little sleep the past few days. Quincannon made himself comfortable on one of the chairs, taking time to load and light his pipe before speaking. Enjoying himself, as he always did at such moments as these.

"Well, Quincannon?" Crowley said irritably. "Don't dally — get on with it."

He did so, though not until he had the briar drawing to his satisfaction. He began by recounting in detail the afternoon's events and reiterating the comments he'd made to Price in the muster room. The three officers listened without interruption, Crowley's expression grim, Price's intently thoughtful, Gentry's skeptical.

When Quincannon paused to relight his pipe, it was the chief who spoke first. "What made you first suspect Mock Quan?"

"His vainglorious attitude and his attempts to lay the blame for the body snatching on Little Pete, when I spoke to him at the Hip Sing Company. Later I discovered James Scarlett had been keeping company with a highborn Chinese woman named Dongmei, that she had likely been the one to introduce him to opium, and that she was a known consort of Mock Quan. It seemed likely then that he had arranged the seduction in order to force Scarlett not only to work on behalf of the Hip Sing but to do his private bidding as well."

"You have proof of this, Quincannon?" Gentry demanded. "It seems pretty far-fetched to me."

"Specific proof, no. But Mock Quan's other actions make it undeniable that he's guilty of murder, attempted murder, body snatching, and racketeering."

"Murder? Whose murder?"

"James Scarlett, of course."

Crowley said, "You mean he ordered the assassination?"

"No. I mean he carried it out himself."

"What's that? You told us before that it was a highbinder who shot Scarlett."

Price was much quicker to understand. "Ah, you mean the assassin was Mock Quan in his coolie disguise. But how can you be sure of that?"

Quincannon told of the shooter wearing a hat with a red topknot, stating it as a known fact from the first and skipping over the manner in which he'd come to the conclusion. "That was the first time he tried to ventilate me, after he shot Scarlett."

"For what reason? How could he have known you were hired to find Scarlett?"

"He didn't," Quincannon said, and went

on to give the theory he had broached to Sabina.

"But then when the attempt on your life failed, why didn't he try again before this afternoon?"

"He saw no need to. When I went to the Hip Sing Company the next morning, he agreed to an audience to find out what, if anything, I knew. Since I made no accusations against him, or said anything that indicated Scarlett might have confided in me, he decided I was not a threat after all — a fatal mistake on his part."

"And Scarlett? Why was he targeted?"

"Likely because he knew too much and couldn't be trusted to keep silent. Knew for one thing that Mock Quan was behind the Bing Ah Kee snatch, the reasons behind it, and the whereabouts of the corpse. How he found out is anyone's guess; he may have been part of the takeover plot from the beginning, or may have simply stumbled on the truth. It's also possible he attempted to blackmail Mock Quan. Scarlett was corrupt enough, and foolish enough, to have thought he could get away with such a trick."

"Sure he was," Gentry said, "but it wasn't Mock Quan he was blackmailing, it was Little Pete. A letter from Scarlett implicating him was found on a highbinder I was forced to shoot yesterday, one of Pete's hatchet men. I saw it myself."

"So I've been told. The letter is a forgery. Planted to throw suspicion on Pete."

"Planted by who? It couldn't have been Mock Quan."

"No, not Mock Quan. Although he did manufacture and plant a similar document to throw suspicion away from him."

"Bullcrap. How do you know that?"

Quincannon explained about his first visit to James Scarlett's law offices, adding by way of a little white lie that he had had permission to do so from his widowed client. "The offices had already been searched sometime earlier that evening," he went on, "or so I believed at the time. The job was done by Mock Quan, not to remove incriminating evidence but to leave the document I mentioned, written in Chinese and inserted in Mock Don Yuen's file."

Price said, "Are you saying he attempted to frame his own father?"

"I am. I had the document translated and it purports to link Scarlett with Mock Don Yuen and Little Pete. Mock Quan is as vicious as they come, with no scruples whatsoever."

"That's nothing but wild speculation," Gentry said. "I still say Pete's the man we're after. Mock Quan is sneaky and ruthless, sure, and he probably does hate his old man, but he's not clever enough to plan a takeover on his own."

"Agreed," Quincannon said. "The plan wasn't his alone. He had help in its devising."

"If he did, it was from Little Pete."

"No, Pete had nothing to do with it."

Crowley snapped, "Well, then, dammit? Who do you say was in it with him?"

"A blue shadow."

"A . . . what? What the devil are you talking about?"

"James Scarlett said two things to me before he died outside the opium resort. One was 'Fowler Alley'; the other was 'blue shadow.' The plain truth is, he was as afraid of a blue shadow as he was of Mock Quan. His wife, though she had no knowledge of it when she came to me, had just as much to fear."

"His wife? Now what're you saying?"

"An attempt was made on Andrea Scarlett's life at her home two nights ago, for the same reason I was targeted in Ross Alley — apprehension that she had been told something damning to the plotters."

The chief sat forward, frowning. "Mock Quan tried to shoot her, too? Why weren't we told about it?"

Quincannon answered the first question, avoiding the second. "It wasn't Mock Quan who fired the shot at Mrs. Scarlett."

"Then who did?"

"His partner in crime, the blue shadow. That is the other thing Scarlett knew that signed his death warrant — the identity of the blue shadow, the man with whom he conspired to cheat justice for accused members of the Hip Sing and who in turn conspired with Mock Quan to establish a criminal empire in Chinatown."

"What partner?" Crowley demanded. "What does 'blue shadow' mean?"

"It means," Quincannon said, "a figure dressed in blue, one whose shadow looms large and has the power to strike fear into the hearts of fools and knaves like James Scarlett. Not a plain blue suit, as the partner wore in the attempted murder of my client, but a blue uniform — a policeman's uniform." He paused dramatically. "One of the men in this room is Mock Quan's accomplice."

All three officers came to their feet as one. Gentry aimed a quivering forefinger as if it were the barrel of his sidearm. "Preposterous nonsense! How dare you accuse one of us —"

"You, Sergeant. I am accusing *you.*"

The smoky air fairly crackled. Price and Crowley were both staring at Gentry; the sergeant's eyes threw sparks at Quincannon. The cords in the short man's neck bulged. His color had become a shade less purple than that of an eggplant.

"It's a dirty lie!" he shouted.

"Cold, hard fact." Quincannon shifted his gaze to Price. "That's the real reason Gentry wanted time alone with Mock Quan downstairs, Lieutenant — not to make him talk, but to make sure he *didn't* talk."

Price said sharply, "Can you prove this allegation?"

"I can, to your and Chief Crowley's satisfaction." Again Quincannon paused for dramatic effect. Sabina was of the stated opinion that the stage had lost a splendid mustache-twirling ham actor when he decided to become a detective. Nonsense, of course, but he forgave her.

"It was Gentry, you'll recall," he said at length, "who constantly urged you and Chief Crowley to crush Little Pete and the Kwong Dock. Gentry who convinced the chief to order the raid on Little Pete's shoe factory. Gentry who killed the highbinder during the raid."

"Yes, by God. Right on all counts."

285

"He tried to put a knife in me!" Gentry cried. "You were there, Lieutenant, you saw it —"

"I saw nothing of the kind. I took your word for it."

"Gentry shot the highbinder," Quincannon said, "for the express purpose of 'finding' the bogus letter that implicated Pete. Didn't you tell me, Lieutenant, that the letter alludes to both Scarlett and Pete knowing the whereabouts of Bing Ah Kee's corpse?"

"That's right, it does."

"Scarlett did know, and so did the sergeant. You'll also recall him saying that night that Little Pete had 'stashed old Bing's bones in cold storage.' Yet for all any of us knew at that point, the body might have been burned, or buried, or weighted and cast into the Bay, or been subjected to any of a dozen other indignities. Why would he use the specific term 'cold storage' unless he knew that was what had been done with the corpse?"

"Lies! Don't listen to him!" Gentry started toward Quincannon with murder in his eye. "Damn you, you're trying to railroad me!"

Price stepped in front of him. "Stand where you are, Sergeant," he said in a voice that brooked no disobedience.

"Then there's the attempt on Mrs. Scarlett's life," Quincannon said. "She had a reasonably good look at the man who tried to kill her and may well be able to identify him." Another stretching of the truth, this, but one that had the desired effect on Price and Crowley, if not on Gentry. The sergeant continued to bluff and bluster.

"It wasn't me!" he cried. "She's another liar if she claims it was!"

"The shot aimed at her was fired at approximately nine P.M. I'll wager you weren't here at the Hall at that time. I'll also wager that you can't provide credible witnesses to your whereabouts. Other than Mrs. Scarlett, that is. Am I correct, Lieutenant?"

"Yes," Price said, "you are. He was away on unspecified business and returned not long before you arrived."

"Lawless business that also included the search of Scarlett's office, so as to remove and destroy any incriminating material that the lawyer might have kept there. And also to filch a sheet of Scarlett's letterhead stationery and some sort of item containing his signature — the tools with which he composed the bogus letter."

The chief stalked around his desk, took a tight grip on Gentry's arm. "A damned highbinder no better than Little Pete or

Mock Quan — is that what you are, Gentry?"

"No! No, I swear —"

"Because if so I'll see your mangy hide strung from the highest flagpole in the city."

Gentry shook his head, sweat glistening slickly on his forehead and cheeks. "I tell you, this damned flycop is trying to frame me. There's no real proof of any of his accusations —"

"Ah, but there is," Quincannon said. "All the evidence needed to, ah, hang your mangy hide from the highest flagpole in the city." What he said next was partly speculation, though he was reasonably sure it was grounded in fact. "When you searched Scarlett's office, you failed to notice and remove several of his case files — cases in which your name is mentioned as a witness in his defense of members of the Hip Sing accused of gambling. In some, it was your testimony, no doubt false or distorted, that resulted in acquittal. In others, it shouldn't be difficult to prove that you suppressed evidence, suborned perjury, or both."

Crowley said grimly, "Are those files still in Scarlett's office?"

"No. They're safely locked away in my office safe. I'll turn them over to you as soon as —"

Gentry called him a vicious name, fumbling his sidearm free of its holster. Price and Quincannon, in rapid consort, prevented him from using it. The lieutenant struck the weapon from his grasp with a fisted thump on the wrist, and Quincannon, with considerable pleasure, fetched the blue shadow a solid blow to the jaw.

While Gentry was being handcuffed by his angry superiors, Quincannon judiciously slipped out of the office and went to find a quiet corner where he could smoke his pipe and enjoy his vindication.

24
SABINA

The twenty-year-old Palace Hotel, also colloquially known as the "Bonanza Inn" and the "Grand Dame of the West," was San Francisco's most luxurious hostelry, far more elegant than the older, second-best Baldwin Hotel in the Uptown Tenderloin. At the time of its construction it had had the distinction of being the largest hotel west of the Mississippi, its many features including 755 guest rooms and suites equipped with private baths, forty-five public and utility rooms, three inner courts, and five redwood-paneled hydraulic elevators referred to by the staff as "rising rooms." Seven floors of white-columned balconies overlooked the open, glass-roofed Grand Central Court which served as a carriage entrance.

Even though she hurried as much as possible, Sabina arrived ten minutes late for the one o'clock appointment with Carson.

Confiscating the $75,000 ransom money, over more of Bertram Blanchford's pathetic pleas, and then transporting it to the agency and locking it away for temporary safekeeping had taken longer than she'd anticipated.

Carson was waiting on the marble-floored promenade, next to one of the columned archways facing the circular carriageway, when she entered the Grand Court. She spied him immediately, a stationary figure among the stream of arriving and departing guests, bellboys with luggage carts, and carriage drivers and their rigs. A smile brightened his handsome face as she approached. As always, he was nattily if conservatively dressed, today in a gray frock coat with matching vest and striped trousers; the gold-headed stick he carried was tucked under one arm. Sabina's heart had skipped a beat the first time she'd seen him, and she'd felt the stirrings of excitement on each of the previous occasions they'd been together, but today she felt nothing other than a faint apprehension. Not even his blue eyes, Stephen's eyes, moved her as they had before.

She allowed him to take her hand in greeting — his touch created no tingling sensations — but not to hold it as he said lightly,

"I was beginning to think I'd been stood up."

"I'm sorry to be late. I was unavoidably detained."

"One of your investigations?"

"Yes. The close of one."

"Satisfactorily closed, I trust."

"For the most part."

His smile dimmed a bit as he studied her. Whatever else he might be, he was also perceptive. "You don't seem particularly happy about it," he said. "Or is it something else that makes you seem so tense and cheerless?"

"I'm afraid so."

"Something to do with me?"

"Unfortunately, yes."

"Oh, I see. The matter of considerable urgency you alluded to in your message."

"Yes."

"Well, then. Shall we discuss whatever it is over luncheon in the American Dining Room?"

"I'd rather not dine, Carson. I'm not particularly hungry."

"Then the matter must be serious, considering your usual fine appetite." He strove for lightness of tone once again, and failed. The smile was gone now, replaced by the shadow of a frown. "It's too public for conversation here. Where would you like to go?"

"There are benches in the garden. One of those will do."

He took her elbow as they moved around to the walkway that led into the tropical garden with its array of exotic plants, statuary, and fountains. Marble benches were set at intervals along the walkway and among the greenery, all presently unoccupied; Carson led her to one of the latter next to a tinkling fountain.

"Well, then," he said when they were seated facing each other. "What's on your mind?"

Sabina had decided to be blunt. Pussyfooting around the subject would only make this more difficult. She said, "The Gold King Mine high-grading scandal eight years ago."

Carson stared at her for several heartbeats, rigidly unmoving, as if he had been temporarily turned to stone. Then his shoulders seemed to sag slightly, and though his gaze held hers, there was hurt in it now. Whether it was old or new pain, she couldn't tell.

"What about the Gold King scandal?" he asked then.

"Were you involved in it in any way?"

"My God. What makes you think that?"

"By your own admission you were employed in the Mother Lode in 1887, in such counties as Amador and such mines as the Gold King. You returned to San Francisco not long after the high grading was exposed and the gang members arrested. You were well acquainted with one of the principals in the scheme, George M. Kinney, a friend and business associate of your father."

"That's hardly evidence of complicity in the crime. You must know that my name was never connected to the Gold King conspiracy. Lord, Sabina, do you always investigate your prospective beaux?"

"Not unless I have cause."

"What cause in this matter? What led you to poke around in my past, to suspect me of wrongdoing?"

"It was brought to my attention that you were being blackmailed by another ringleader recently released from prison, Artemas Sneed."

Carson winced. "Brought to your attention by whom?"

"The man who calls himself S. Holmes."

"Holmes? I don't know anyone by that name."

"He has used others on occasion. Tall, spare, middle-aged, with a thin, hawkish nose and a prominent chin. Speaks with a pronounced British accent."

"I've never met anyone who answers that description. How on earth would he know of the Gold King and Artemas Sneed?"

A very good question. One I intend to ask Mr. S. Holmes if our paths cross again.

"You haven't answered my question, Carson," she said. "Were you involved in any way in the gold-stealing? And please don't lie to me. I'll know it if you do."

He said nothing for a time, both hands tightly clasping the gold handle of his stick. Then he let out a breath and said resignedly, "All right. I'll tell you the absolute truth. The answer is yes — and no."

"What does that mean?"

"It means that I was involved, yes, but only briefly and indirectly. I took no active part in the thefts, received not a single penny of the proceeds from the stolen gold. I was fortunate — my name was never brought up because so far as Kinney and the others knew, they had no cause to bring me down with them. I was never part of the gang."

"Then in what way were you involved?"

"Kinney came up to Amador just after I was hired by the Gold King's owners and attempted to recruit me," Carson said with some bitterness. "I had no idea he was a crook until then — it was a shock to learn that he was. He'd had heavy stock-market setbacks and was in dire need of cash, his excuse for having orchestrated the scheme. Sneed was his first recruit, I was to be his second."

"To do what, exactly?"

"Falsify my reports on new and established veins, to make it seem as though there were not as much gold-bearing ore in certain sections of the Gold King as there was. That would have made it easier for Sneed and his crew to steal and smuggle out the richest dust. For doing this I was to be paid five thousand dollars in cash."

"Did you agree to it?"

"Not in the beginning. I turned Kinney down at first, but he kept after me — he could be very persuasive. Finally, at a meeting with Kinney and Sneed, and under the influence of several drinks of forty-rod whiskey, I weakened and gave in to temptation. To my everlasting shame."

"Your family is rich," Sabina said. "Did you really need the five thousand dollars?"

"No, except that I was young and foolish and independent as the devil, and I hated having to ask my father for money. My salary in those days was not large and I . . . well, the mining camps were rough-and-ready places and I admit to a weakness for poker in those days." Carson's mouth quirked self-deprecatingly. "And to a fondness for sowing more than my share of wild oats."

"Did you falsify your Gold King reports?"

"No. I came to my senses in time, thank God."

"Kinney and Sneed must have been upset when you told them."

"I didn't tell them. I pretended to follow through, but in fact all I did was prepare two reports — a false one to satisfy them without actually aiding in the thefts, and a genuine, completely honest one for the Gold King's owners."

"Did you accept the five thousand dollars?"

Carson shook his head. "I told Kinney my conscience wouldn't allow it. He said I was a fool, but he didn't argue; he was only too happy to keep the five thousand for himself."

A trio of hotel guests came hurrying along the promenade from the carriage entrance, chattering loudly among themselves. Sabina waited until they passed before she said, "If you came to your senses in time, why did you pretend to do Kinney's bidding? Why didn't you simply go to the owners or the authorities and reveal the plot to them?"

"I did, though not directly. I am the author of the anonymous letter that led to the gang's exposure and arrest." Carson's tone was bitter again, this time with self-recrimination. "My conscience finally got the better of me after I moved on to Grass Valley, but I didn't have the courage to go back and expose the scheme in person — I was afraid of being arrested myself and sent to prison, of blackening the Montgomery name. So I settled for writing the letter. God knows, I should have done it sooner."

"If you had," Sabina said, "someone in the gang might have realized you were responsible and implicated you."

"I almost wish that had happened. As it was, I returned to San Francisco and accepted an offer to join Monarch Engineering. But I lived on tenterhooks during the trial and for a long time afterward. Eventually I came to believe my past mistake would remain buried, and so it was until that devil Sneed was released from prison."

"He'd found out somehow that you wrote the anonymous letter?"

"Guessed it. A man has a lot of time to think when he's cooped up in a cell for eight years, he said."

"Did you deny it?"

"I tried to when he first turned up at my

office, the day before you and I dined at Haquette's, but he just laughed. I suppose he could tell from my reactions that he'd guessed correctly. He threatened to expose me, to make my part in the high grading seem much worse than it was, unless I paid him the same amount Kinney offered me — five thousand dollars."

"Did you give him the money?"

"No. Not one red cent."

Sabina raised an eyebrow.

"God's honest truth," Carson said. "I told him I refused to be blackmailed and in turn threatened him with a charge of attempted extortion."

"You thought no one would believe the word of an ex-convict, eight years after the fact?"

"I hoped that might be the case. But that's not why I refused to pay blackmail. I escaped punishment for what I did and almost did in Amador County, but my actions have weighed on my conscience ever since. There would be greater shame in accommodating a man like Sneed to keep my past sins secret than in having them revealed and my reputation sullied. It would almost be a relief to have the truth come out. My only regret if it does is what it would do to my father and the Montgomery family name."

"Did Sneed make any further attempt to blackmail you?"

Carson nodded. "He slunk away that first time, but then two nights ago he showed up at my home with the same demand and an additional threat. If I didn't pay, he would not only ruin me by going to the newspapers, he would see to it that I suffered a serious, possibly fatal 'accident.'"

Two nights ago. The evening the bughouse Sherlock had summoned her to Huntington Park. He must have expected Sneed to come calling at the Montgomery mansion, perhaps even followed him there.

"And your answer then?" she asked.

"The same as before: no. I made him aware that I wasn't afraid of him and cast him out."

"Was that the truth? That you weren't afraid of him?"

"Yes. I encountered more than a few men like Sneed in the mining camps. Full of bluff and bluster, but cowards at heart."

This, and the rest of what Carson had said thus far, had the ring of truth. Sabina had watched him closely and he'd exhibited none of the telltale signs of the liar: no nervous gestures, or facial tics, or averted or too direct eye contact; no glib or overly earnest statements, no points glossed over or contradictory. But his innocence or guilt in the death of Artemas Sneed was yet to be determined.

Sabina was aware of water splashing in the fountain behind them, of the scents from the exotic blooms — her senses heightening as she pressed on with her questioning. "Did you see Sneed again after that night at your home?"

"No. I assume he gave up and crawled back into whatever hole he's living in."

"The Wanderer's Rest on Davis Street."

No reaction from Carson except mild surprise.

"You didn't know he was lodging there?"

"No. It isn't likely he'd want me to know."

"That stick of yours," Sabina said. "It wouldn't happen to contain a removable steel shaft, would it?"

He blinked, taken aback by the apparent non sequitur. "You mean a sword cane? No, of course not."

"Do you own such a stick?"

"No. I've never carried any weapon except a pistol, and that only during my time in the Mother Lode. What does a sword cane have to do with the matter at hand?"

"It's the instrument that was used to kill Artemas Sneed."

"To kill — Sneed is dead?"

"Run through in his room. Perhaps murdered, more likely killed in self-defense during a struggle. There was an unfired pistol in his hand."

"My good Christ." Carson's astonishment, she was sure, was genuine. "How do you know all this, Sabina?"

"I have my sources." She was not about to admit that she had discovered the body, or that she had failed to inform the police.

"And you think that I may have — No, I swear by all that's holy, it wasn't me. I've never been to Davis Street in my life."

"Then you won't mind telling me where you were between five and seven last evening."

"Is that when Sneed was killed? I was at the Bank Exchange in the Montgomery Block, imbibing too many of Duncan Nichols's Pisco Punches with three of my firm's clients. If you'd like their names —"

Sabina shook her head. There was no need; Carson could not have a more credible alibi.

He said after a short silence, "Who did kill Sneed, I wonder?"

"It could be anyone. An ex-convict, would-be extortionist, and habitué of the Barbary Coast is sure to have made enemies, in and out of prison. The police may never find out."

"Do they have my name?"

"No. Nor will they have it from me."

"My part in the high-grading scheme . . . do you intend to tell the authorities about that?"

"You've given me no reason to. You had no direct role in the conspiracy, and you were responsible for the arrest and punishment of the perpetrators. Legally you couldn't be prosecuted in any event. The statute of limitations on theft-related crimes is seven years. So you needn't worry — as far as I'm concerned, your family's good name and yours are secure."

"I'm in your debt." Then, "But what do you honestly think, Sabina? Do I deserve punishment for what I did?"

"You have been punished," she said, "for the past eight years. I imagine you'll continue to be for the rest of your days."

"By my conscience, you mean."

"Yes."

"And rightly so." He reached out in a tentative way to press fingertips against her arm, then withdrew his hand quickly as if afraid his touch might have offended her. "Your opinion of me matters a great deal," he said. "I believe you know that. Have you lost feeling and respect for me, now that you know the truth about my past?"

Sabina looked into his blue, Stephen-like eyes and again felt none of the once-strong attraction. She said slowly, "That isn't an easy question to answer."

"Please be truthful. You don't feel quite the same, do you?"

"Perhaps not."

"And you'd rather not have anything more to do with me."

"I can't say right now, Carson. I do know I'd prefer not to attend the performance at the Baldwin tomorrow evening, or to share any more dinners in the immediate future."

"I understand."

There was nothing more to be said. They stood as one and without speaking left the Grand Court and then the hotel. At the bridge that spanned New Montgomery and connected with the Grand Hotel across the street, his parting smile was melancholy, his good-bye handshake weak, his step slow and ponderous as he left her. Watching after him, she couldn't help wondering if this was the last she would ever see of Carson Montgomery.

25
QUINCANNON

Quincannon finished regaling Sabina with a somewhat embellished account of his role in defusing the Chinatown powder keg by saying, "Gentry's shell was no harder to crack than a Dungeness crab's. It took Crowley and Price less than fifteen minutes to break him wide open."

"Doubtless with the aid of some not so gentle persuasion."

"Have you ever known the police to use another kind on a treacherous renegade?"

She smiled and took a sip of her tea. Quincannon gazed fondly at her across the white linen tablecloth with its red rose in the center between them. It was Saturday noon and they were seated in the rather intimate atmosphere of the Maison Riche at Dupont and Geary Streets, one of the city's tonier French bistros, whose dinner specialties included such epicurean delights as *caviar sur canane* and *poulet de grain au cresson.* The luncheon fare, in Quincannon's opinion, was no less elegant, even if the portions were on the skimpy side.

He was in high good spirits today. It was not often he was able to persuade Sabina to dine with him, and he had anticipated yet another turndown when he broached the subject at the agency the previous afternoon. Her acceptance had surprised and delighted him, the more so because it had been neither slow in coming nor apparently grudging.

Her present mood, however, was less ebullient than his. She seemed quiet and introspective, he thought, though she was nonetheless splendid company outside the business confines of Carpenter and Quincannon, Professional Detective Services. He hadn't asked what was troubling her, sensing that she wouldn't have told him. Carson Montgomery again, mayhap? Perhaps, but her acceptance of the luncheon invitation was a sign, or so he fervently hoped, that she might not be as enamored of the socialite as he'd feared.

She said as she lowered her cup, "Gentry's motive, I imagine, was power and greed, the same as Mock Quan's."

"Those, and an obsessive passion for the services of flower willows, a vice he shared with James Scarlett. An endless supply of beautiful courtesans, Dongmei among them, was the reason he joined forces with Mock Quan in the first place, just as opium and Dongmei were the sources of Scarlett's corruption."

"A police sergeant and the Western-educated son of a tong president — strange bedfellows."

"And a pair of incompetent bughouse fools, else all of Chinatown might be in the midst of a bloodbath by now."

"Yes. Another crisis averted."

"For the time being, anyway. Until another, more stable Mock Quan emerges or someone else lights the fuse — some cold-blooded hound like Little Pete. Mark my words. One of these days, the whole Quarter will go up in flames."

"You may be right. In any event, it's a relief to mark this case closed — particularly for Mrs. Scarlett."

Quincannon concurred. After leaving the Hall of Justice the day before, he had gone to Elizabeth Petrie's home on Clay Street to give their client the news. Andrea Scarlett had been weepingly grateful that she need no longer fear for her life and could return to her home; the arrest of her husband's murderer and her would-be assassin seemed much less important to her. Understandable, if a bit on the callous side.

Sabina took a bite of her *salade de crevettes*. And then nearly caused him to drop his fork by saying, "I've been thinking that we should waive the rest of Mrs. Scarlett's fee. I'll include a letter to that effect with our final report — Why are you looking at me that way?"

"Waive her fee?" he said, aghast. "What put that daft notion in your head?"

"It's the least we can do for the woman. She may not be the most virtuous person, but neither is she wicked. She has had a trying time, and she's a widow with insufficient funds to support herself, much less pay us. She will surely have to return to her former work as a seamstress. Seamstresses, whether you're aware of it or not, are not at all well paid."

Quincannon made a pained sound in his beard. "Sabina, have you forgotten that I was shot at by Mock Quan on two separate occasions and nearly killed both times? Not to mention made to trek through low Chinatown alleys, prowl opium dens, invade an undertaking parlor in search of a snatched corpse —"

"Don't be melodramatic. Of course I haven't forgotten."

"Well, then? All of that, not to mention a near tarnish on our reputation as detectives, for not so much as a copper cent?"

"We have Mrs. Scarlett's retainer —"

"A mere pittance."

"— and we'll hardly miss the remaining few hundred dollars. It's the proper thing to do and you know it."

"I know nothing of the kind."

"Well, it is," Sabina said. "Just as not telling Mrs. Harriet Blanchford what her son did is the proper thing to do."

"What's that? According to your account, Bertram Blanchford is a nasty piece of work — lower than a gopher's hind end. He deserves whatever punishment comes his way."

"Yes, but the old woman doesn't deserve to suffer any more than she already has. She is still grieving over the loss of her husband, and relieved and happy to have him back in his final resting place. The truth about Bertram would make a misery of the rest of her days."

"Is that why you've yet to return the ransom money to her?"

"Yes. I'll do that once I've invented a story to explain how I came by it and who is responsible."

"And what if Bertram should try another

309

scheme to dupe money from her?"

"I daresay he won't. Not after I put the fear of God into him."

"He'll still stand to inherit when she passes on."

"The bookmakers and sure-thing men who hold his markers may not allow him to live that long," Sabina said. "Billy the Bookie has an evil reputation. But if Bertram survives with nothing more than a beating or two, Harriet Blanchford is no fool. She knows of his profligate ways and she may not trust him with what remains of the Blanchford fortune. In any event, that is her business. Ours is to spare her any more grief."

"And to collect our due for services rendered. You don't intend to waive any of our fee in *her* case, do you?"

"No, of course not. And a not inconsiderable one it is, you'll be pleased to note. Five hundred dollars, plus expenses."

Quincannon admitted that this was a sizable sum. In other circumstances it might not have completely made up for a loss of the Scarlett fee, but here in the Maison Riche, with Sabina for company and on the table in front of him one of his favorite dishes, *foie de veau aux oignons,* the fattening of their bank balance seemed not quite as important as it usually did. He was, in fact, reasonably content with his lot and that of Carpenter and Quincannon, Professional Detective Services. And would be even more so if he knew the precise nature of Sabina's relationship with Carson Montgomery, past and present.

Should he take the bull by the horns, as it were, and bring up the subject here and now, admit to what he'd been told by Theodore Bonesall? There might not be a more propitious time or place than over a congenial luncheon in a crowded restaurant.

He was considering this when Sabina surprised him by broaching the subject herself, almost as if she had been reading his mind. "I spoke to Mr. Bonesall at Western States Bank the other day," she said, almost off handedly, "regarding the Blanchford matter. He told me in passing that he'd had a conversation with you about my private life. Evenings spent in the company of Carson Montgomery, to be specific."

Quincannon was at a loss for words. All he could manage was, "Ahh."

"You know all too well how I feel about that sort of thing, John."

"Yes, but . . . ah, Bonesall happened to mention seeing you and Mr., ah, Montgomery dining together at the Old Poodle Dog, so naturally I was a trifle curious —"

"Naturally. And your trifling curiosity has led you to speculate about my relationship with Carson ever since."

"Well, now . . ."

"I am not now nor have I ever been romantically involved with Mr. Montgomery in any way," Sabina said in her no-nonsense voice. "Does that put your mind at ease?"

"My dear Sabina, I never once imagined —"

"Oh, bosh. Admit it — you've been fretting for days over the possibility that Carson and I have been having illicit relations. Well, we haven't. As a matter of fact, you might as well know that we are no longer keeping company. Now will you be so good as to stop prying?"

He could barely contain his elation. Not romantically involved! Dinner companions, nothing more! No longer seeing Mr. Montgomery!

"You have my solemn promise," he said. He savored a tender forkful of calf's liver and onions before he added, "But may I ask a consideration in return?"

"That depends on what it is."

"Now that your evenings are free again, and in deference to my deep affection for you, I would take it as a great personal favor if you relaxed your rule against fraternization and permitted me the privilege of acting as your escort on occasion — not only for luncheons such as this but for an evening's meal and entertainment. Just that, nothing more."

She regarded him unblinkingly for such a long while that he felt sure she would decline, perhaps even launch into another of her business-only speeches. But bless her, she did neither. She sighed softly and said, "Very well. But only if you swear to make no advances, to behave as a gentleman."

"At all times," he said. "Oh, at all times."

He meant it, too.

For the nonce anyway. For the nonce . . .

26
SABINA

She was enjoying a quietly relaxing evening in her rooms, curled up with Adam, a glass of white wine, and a copy of the *Police Gazette* (Cousin Callie would have been horrified at her choice of reading matter), when the door buzzer sounded.

That had better not be another messenger, she thought. Or a solicitor, although it was late for that breed to come calling. Not Carson, surely. John, attempting to take immediate advantage of her moment of weakness at Maison Riche? If it was John, she would not only recant, but give him a severe tongue-lashing.

But it wasn't John. Or Carson. Her caller was the alleged Mr. S. Holmes.

"Good evening, Mrs. Carpenter," he said, bowing. He wore his Sherlock outfit tonight — gray cape, deerstalker cap. In one hand he carried the blackthorn walking stick; tucked under his other arm was a small wicker basket. "I trust I haven't come at an inopportune time?"

"No. But I must say I'm surprised to see you here after what you said to me three nights ago."

"What I said? Ah, that I consider it unseemly for a gentleman to visit a lady in her quarters past nightfall. That is my usual policy, especially when a game is afoot. However, now that I am temporarily unencumbered again, I deemed it expedient to present myself in person. In point of fact I have a gift for you."

"Gift?"

"A small token of my esteem for you and your skill in the practice of our noble profession. May I enter for a few moments?"

Sabina nodded and stepped aside. The Englishman swept off his cap as he entered the vestibule, stood there for a moment looking past her into the front parlor. "Charming quarters," he said. "Quite befitting a woman of your taste and station."

"I'm honored by your approval," she said dryly.

He extended the wicker basket. "With my compliments, dear lady."

It was somewhat heavier than it looked, and she felt movement inside. When she lifted the lid, she was looking at an all-black kitten. It peered up at her with enormous amber-colored eyes, mewed as if saying hello.

Her heart melted to it instantly. It seemed to feel the same toward her; it began to purr, flexing its tiny paws, when she picked it up and cuddled it against her breast. Its fur was as soft as eiderdown.

"As per your wishes, a playmate for your Abyssinian-Siamese mix — Adam by name, if memory serves. You're pleased with my choice of a black short-haired female?"

Yes, she was — pleased, surprised, and touched. "Very much," she said, stroking the kitten's back. Adam would be, too, she hoped. "I don't know what to say, except thank you."

"That will do splendidly. Unlike Adam, you see, this little beggar will not shed hairs upon your clothing."

"Does she have a name?"

"Not yet. That is for you to decide."

"Perhaps I'll name her after you."

"I would be honored."

Not necessarily. Two names came immediately to mind, "Crackbrain" and "Beelzebub," though of course she could hardly saddle the poor kitten with either one.

"How did you know I was interested in a playmate for Adam?" she asked him.

The Englishman's only reply was his infuriatingly enigmatic smile.

"Carson Montgomery is the only person I mentioned it to," Sabina said. "But he claims not to know you at all."

"That is the truth. We have never met vis-à-vis."

"Do you still have him under surveillance?"

"No. That is what I meant in saying I am no longer encumbered — my inquiries concerning Mr. Montgomery have ceased. As have yours, I trust, now that he is no longer threatened by his minimal involvement in the Gold King scandal. Or by the villainous Artemas Sneed."

"Why is Sneed no longer a threat?"

"Come, come, Mrs. Carpenter, you mustn't try to fence with me. You know perfectly well that the man died a violent death two nights ago, having yourself discovered his body at the Wanderer's Rest."

She blinked at him. "How do you know that?"

"I have my sources, as you have yours."

That was almost the same thing she'd said to Carson at the Palace Hotel. Holmes's claim seemed equally valid, annoyingly so. Whereas it had taken her and John years of combined activity to compile their various sources, the Englishman had managed to develop his in less than a year of residence in the city and without any official standing. How he'd accomplished this by flitting about in the shadowy underworld on mysterious missions was as astonishing as it was inexplicable.

"Ah, yes," he continued in his self-aggrandizing fashion, "my brain attic is filled with a vast array of knowledge. Else how would I have earned my reputation as the world's finest detective?"

"Oh, indeed," Sabina said, but as always he was immune to sarcasm. "Will you at least tell me how you found out about Carson's past and Sneed's attempt at blackmail, and why you took it upon yourself to investigate?"

That dratted smile again. But this time he deigned to give her an answer of sorts. "One trained in the finer points of observation and ratiocination learns much in places such as Soho in my homeland and the Barbary Coast in this otherwise fair city."

"So you were shadowing Carson in an attempt to save him from Sneed? Or was it Sneed you were after?"

"All criminals and their nefarious deeds are grist for the mill of Sherlock Holmes. Including your Mr. Montgomery, if he had proven to be more culpable eight years ago than he was."

"He's not my Mr. Montgomery."

"Ah? Your liaison with him has ended?"

"That is none of your concern, Mr. Holmes."

"Indubitably not. But if you and the gentleman have come to a parting of the ways, perhaps it is for the best. I have long felt that the estimable if somewhat contentious Mr. Quincannon would make a fitting suitor as well as a worthy business partner."

The insufferable cheek of the man! The kitten kept her from making an angry retort by mewing, curling a paw around one of her fingers and then nipping with sharp little teeth.

"I should say the little beggar is hungry," Holmes said. "A spot of milk or cream would seem to be in order."

Sabina nodded, still not trusting herself to speak.

"And I must be off. Duty calls." He replaced his cap, turned to open the door. Outside on the stoop, he said, "I really am quite pleased that you like my gift, dear lady."

"Yes. Thank you again."

"Not at all. My pleasure." He bowed. "I expect we shall see each other again before

I return to England. Until then, *au revoir.*"

Sabina watched him walk away at a jaunty pace, his stick tapping on the flagstones. The kitten had been a thoughtful gesture, yes, and she was grateful, but Lord, she fervently hoped never to cross the Englishman's path again. If he ever did leave San Francisco, it wouldn't be soon enough to suit her.

She carried the purring kitten — what would she name her? Eve, perhaps? — into the kitchen and introduced her to Adam before pouring out a saucer of cream. Adam and the new addition to the household seemed to take to each other right away, just as she'd hoped. Yes, Eve was the proper name. Adam and Eve.

It was while she was watching Eve lap cream that an afterimage of the bogus Sherlock's jaunty, stick-tapping departure popped into her mind, bringing with it a sudden belated suspicion. It hadn't been Carson he'd been spying on, any more than it had been her. It had, all along, been Artemas Sneed. Suppose, then, he had decided to confront Sneed about the attempted blackmail. Suppose that blackthorn stick of his was not solid wood, but in fact contained a concealed weapon such as a long, sharp sword.

Suppose it was the bogus Mr. Holmes who had skewered Sneed in his room at the Wanderer's Rest.

Possible, entirely possible. He was shrewd enough to have successfully copied his idol's methods of observation and deduction; he might also have adopted a form of self-protection he believed the real Sherlock employed, and not been hesitant to use it if the need arose.

But whether or not that was the true explanation, it was moot. He would never tell. And she, alas, would never know.

ABOUT THE AUTHORS

Marcia Muller is the *New York Times* bestselling creator of private investigator Sharon McCone. The author of more than thirty-five novels, Muller received the Mystery Writers of America's Grand Master Award in 2005.

Bill Pronzini, creator of the Nameless Detective, is a highly praised novelist, short-story writer, and anthologist. He received the Grand Master Award from the Mystery Writers of America in 2008, making Muller and Pronzini the only living couple to share the award.